Dorothea's Daughter

and other nineteenth-century postscripts

by Barbara Hardy

D1501476

Victorian Secrets 2011

Published by

Victorian Secrets Limited
32 Hanover Terrace
Brighton BN2 9SN

www.victoriansecrets.co.uk

Dorothea's Daughter and Other Nineteenth-Century Postscripts
by Barbara Hardy

Composition and design by Catherine Pope
Cover image © iStockphoto.com/whitemay
Cover background © iStockphoto.com/khorzhevska

A catalogue record for this book is available from the British Library.

ISBN 978-1-906469-24-5

For my daughters, Julia and Kate Hardy

Contents

Acknowledgements

I am very grateful to William Baker, Janet El-Rayess, Lucy Ellmann, Graham Handley, Debbie Harrison, Sam Hynes, Sybil Oldfield, Sue Roe, Jennifer Tanner, and my students in the Creative Writing MA at Sussex University, for help and inspiration.

About Barbara Hardy

Barbara Hardy has been a literary critic for over fifty years, specialising in the Victorian novel, theory of narrative and lyric, but also writing studies of Shakespeare, Jane Austen, and Dylan Thomas. Her recent books on George Eliot and Dickens continue the close analysis – once out of fashion but coming back – which has always marked her work, with an fresh emphasis on the artist's explicit and implicit analysis of creativity. She has published many reviews and articles, two books of poetry, a memoir and a novel, teaches and takes workshops, and is interested in the crossover of literary criticism and creative writing. She is working on Elizabeth Gaskell and a sequence of poems about Dante.

Barbara Hardy is Professor Emeritus at Birkbeck, University of London, Honorary Professor at Swansea, University of Wales, Fellow of the British Academy, the Royal Society of Literature, and the Universities of Wales, Swansea, Swansea Metropolitan, Royal Holloway, and Birkbeck, and an Honorary Member of the Modern Languages Association.

Preface

This is a collection of short stories based on novels by Jane Austen, Charlotte Brontë, Dickens, George Eliot, and Thomas Hardy. I call them postscripts rather than sequels because although they enter into dialogues with the original narratives by dwelling on suggestions not developed in the novels, and detain the characters for a little while after the end of their story, they respect the authors' conclusions -- the deaths, marriages, births and reconciliations which form the grand finales in nineteenth-century novels. Some readers find any kind of sequel intrusive, but I am not making additions to the novelists' work or changing the pattern, only drawing the eye to artistic detail, or drawing out loose threads in the original fabric to weave a little new material.

My stories are primarily, but not wholly, concerned with women characters. I imagine the continuing relations of Emma Knightley and her old rival Jane Fairfax as married women, the reflections and memories of Fanny (in *Mansfield Park*) after her marriage to Edmund Bertram, and the development and prospects of her sister Susan Price. I return to Paulina Bretton and Lucy Snowe (of *Villette*) and to Little Dorrit, as they respond to fresh stimulus, in ways which imagine change but endorse their appearances in the novels. These inventions lightly question simplifications in the original happy endings, suggesting that the friendship of Emma and Jane would remain an imperfect one, and speculating that Mary Crawford's ghost might haunt Fanny's sensitive memory, after the live and lively Mary is banished to clinch a moral and clear the way for Fanny's happy marriage. I feel sure that Amy Dorrit's keen memory and introspection, like Fanny's, would now and then call up a few troubling fancies for her happy-ever-after as Mrs Clennam. These postscripts do not quarrel with the novelist, but reflect a little on the endings.

The novelist may gloss over, ignore or be insensitive to something which appears crucial, particularly to a modern reader, for political, psychological or aesthetic reasons, and I have returned to several characters or events which seem to me ambiguously concluded or left incomplete.

I follow the career of Harriet Beadle (or Tattycoram), whose real name many readers forget, into a future beyond the end of *Little Dorrit*, where she is polished off rather glibly and sentimentally by Dickens, and I have let her assert her earlier pride and vitality.

I re-consider the attitude of Jane Rochester (once Jane Eyre) and that of her husband, to Adèle Varens, who may or may not be Rochester's illegitimate child, and about whom he told a psychologically plausible but incoherent story to Jane: the Rochesters' feeling towards her would almost certainly be affected by their marriage and the birth of their own child in ways the novelist does not envisage, and which disturb the idea of a perfected affinity.

The stories and fates of Lucy Snowe and Paulina Bretton are linked by Charlotte Brontë in a strong antithesis, and I wanted to shift and complicate the polarity a little, have another look at Lucy's independence, do justice to Paulina's likely capacity for growth, and reconsider the novel's so-called open ending.

Mr. Dombey's feelings about his second wife Edith, and his awareness of her dead son (forgotten by many readers) are omitted from the novel's happy-ever-after conclusion, in spite of his climactic moral conversion, his reconciliation with his daughter Florence, and Edith's own final interview with Florence. I have supplied a dialogue which fills a gap in Dickens's subtle portrayal of unhappy marriage, and continues the remarkable conversation initiated by Edith before she leaves the Dombey house and flees to France.

Observing aspects of Lucy Deane as they are mutedly presented in *The Mill on the Floss*, I ask, adapting George Eliot's question about Dorothea in *Middlemarch*, 'Why always Maggie Tulliver?' and suggest that dark Maggie's blonde cousin, also simplified, but not cramped, in a formal antithesis, is a character not so different from her tragic cousin as she may appear, and likely to be affected by the drowning of her cousins in ways undeveloped in the novel. The 'sweet face' at Maggie's tomb, at the end, is generally taken to be Lucy's but is tactfully not identified, so I felt free to emphasise the ambiguity of the image, without ruling out the usual interpretation.

I have followed Angel Clare and 'Liza-Lu a short way on their journey after the execution of Tess, in *Tess of the Durbervilles*, reflecting on their response to Tess's last wish for them, which Hardy impresses on our imagination at the end of his great bitter novel: her thought of their marriage is her image of peace and healing, but not conclusive, and I wanted to place it more emphatically as the tragic heroine's hope rather than the novelist's panacea. I retain Hardy's final image of Angel and 'Liza-Lu as the sad companionable pair but make a space for 'Liza-Lu, like her sister, to assert her identity.

It is not only women who assert themselves dynamically in my postscripts. Brontë's Rochester and Dickens's Dombey are questioned in their patriarchal roles by conversation with imaginative women, with different results. And I have taken a little further Philip Wakem's comment, in his letter to Maggie near the end of the novel, that his love for her may nourish and enlarge his imagination and his art, and have linked his assertion of identity and purpose with Lucy Deane's development.

George Eliot tells us nothing about Dorothea's daughter, (whom most readers seem not to notice, though attentive readers should infer that she is born) and I have used this invisible woman, least developed of all the characters I have re-imagined, for my book's title as well as for a new story.

I have invented moments in the future lives of all these characters, who are realistic and complex enough to have futures – futures which the novels leave dark or temptingly open to fresh development or commentary. The characters are revived, and their identities asserted, in imaginary conversations in which the original story is modified or extended but also – in essentials – confirmed. My narratives try to jump the historical gap which separates us from their novels to develop suggestion, to fill in lacunae, and occasionally to argue a little with the novelist, but I hope not to make anachronistic quibbbles or lose historical sense and distance.

The stories turn on the problems of being a woman – as I have said, not separable from the problems of being a man, as is clear in Rochester, Dombey and Wakem – problems in some ways particular to their historical period but highly relevant to our own times. The subject of woman's struggling consciousness and assertion runs through all the narratives, and I hope makes the collection more than a sum of its parts.

I am attempting a critique in the form of short fiction, using a language which is not imitative of period or authors but which tries not to clash with the original styles. I am imagining possibilities, not improvements, and I hope my *hommage* and critical reconstruction will send readers back to the novels, which I love, admire, and have read many times, several in childhood.

Each story is headed by an extract or extracts from the novel, setting the context, and where it has seemed useful, reminding readers of plot, action, or nuance. Most stories are followed by a brief note, reminding readers of problematic, unobtrusive, or forgotten features, explaining and expanding implications, and sometimes making explicit my reasons for writing the postscript.

Twilight in Mansfield Parsonage

... Susan remained to supply her place – Susan became the stationary niece – delighted to be so! – and equally well adapted for it by a readiness of mind, and an inclination for usefulness, as Fanny had been by sweetness of temper, and strong feelings of gratitude. From Chapter 17 of *Mansfield Park* by Jane Austen

Fanny put another log on the parlour fire and Susan bent forward to hold her hands to the warmth, then leaned back against her cushions, smiling at her sister.

'Ah, Fanny, this is comfortable, as dear Aunt would say. Comfortable – I think that is her favourite word. The children are asleep in their little beds, safe and sound, Edmund ridden off like the good conscientious clergyman he is, to see poor old Goodman, and kind Sir Thomas is taking my usual place beside Aunt, Pug and their sofa, so that you and I may have this evening together. It is an unusual pleasure, Fanny, for us to be alone, and for once not occupied, is it not? I am glad you have no working candles. You see, I have not brought any work with me, but pray do not reproach me with idleness. To be together like this brings back those old times in Portsmouth when we used to escape from all the noise in the parlour and sit in our room upstairs, talking and reading together. I remember that we had no fire in that cold little room, but we did not mind the cold, did we? I was finding the warmth of a sister's love.'

'Ah, Susan, so was I. So was I. And since you have come to Mansfield and I have seen you blossoming and becoming a good useful woman, in every way that could be desired, I have grown to cherish a sister and a sister's love to the full.'

'It is like you to say so. But I should never have settled here so happily had it not been for you and your help. Yes, that bare little room in the small house in Portsmouth – so cramped and so noisy a house, so unlike Mansfield and this dear parsonage – was where I first learnt to know you and to love you, and to learn so many things from you – like speaking quietly, and being more patient, like you. I often recall those times. Do you too, Fanny? In your full and busy life?'

'How could I ever forget them? I remember them well. I remember how I looked forward to coming back home, to Mama and all of you, after the long years of separation. I remember how I arrived at the Portsmouth house and felt lost and unhappy, especially after William joined his ship. I was so startled by Father. Even after I grew used to everything and everyone I often felt sad and oppressed, even shocked, but I was happy to become acquainted with you and talk to you about dear Mansfield, for which I was so homesick.'

'Yes, I remember you amazed me by your gentle manner and thoughtful ways, so unlike my impetuous blundering! And I was so impressed and astonished by your knowledge, and the books you got from the library. I had never heard anyone quote poetry before. "She longed intensely for her home": I blush to remember how in my ignorance I thought they were your own words, and you smiled, but most kindly, dear Fanny, and you talked to me about poetry, and read to me, and helped me understand – just a little – your liking for

Cowper. But I was late coming to books, as you know. Unlike you, I am not a reader, and unlike you I have no great understanding of poems, but I can never forget that line about being homesick, which you quoted with tears in your eyes.'

'Ah, yes, I was homesick indeed, for dear Mansfield, as I had never expected to be. For weeks I had been indeed been longing intensely to see Mama and all of you. It is good to look back, at all the pains and pleasures of the Portsmouth time, here in the soft twilight, by the bright fire. Our talk was not always so literary and elevated, though, was it? I remember how you liked to hear about Aunt Bertram and Pug and her needle-work. And about dear Edmund. The tales of Mansfield Park. And my own beloved east room – that too was a cold room where I never minded the cold. But then Uncle – kind Uncle – ordered that there should always be a fire lit there for me.'

'Yes, and there always has been, since it became my sitting-room – whenever I want it. I am not as fond of solitude and reading as you were.'

'Ah, we never imagined that one day Mansfield Park would be your own beloved home.'

'No indeed! Little did I think then that I should become adept at carpet-work and fringing and netting, and taking fat old Pug for his short breathless walks in the shrubbery, and piling the cushions on dear Aunt's sofa. And reading the newspaper to Uncle, as I have come to do now his sight has begun to fail. The other night he was good enough to praise my reading. That I owe to your example, Fanny. But Aunt Norris – how reluctant you were to tell me about her, so charitable as you always were. And little did we think then how she would leave Mansfield, so soon after my coming, and forever. Oh dear, how she disliked my arrival, and showed that she did not care for me. And how relieved I was when she went away to live with our cousin. Pray do not think me heartless. It was only that I never met Maria, as you know. Fanny, I hope you do not mind my asking, but has Edmund heard anything of them lately?'

'No, I think he has not. We do not often speak of her but he always tells me when he hears from Maria. He writes to her now and then. I believe he is the only one of the family who does. Uncle asked him to look after their affairs, so that he himself need not correspond with my cousin, or even with Aunt Norris. And Tom was never much of a writer, you know, and he has been away so much.'

The sisters were silent for a little while, each in her different way reflecting on Sir Thomas's implacable shame and his reproach, of others and himself, and of Aunt Norris and their cousin Maria together in unhappy solitude. That would be cold company indeed, Fanny thought; the tears sprang to her eyes, and she was glad of the dim light.

'Fanny, if you do not mind my asking – do you think it possible that poor Maria will ever marry again?'

'I have never thought to ask that question. Of Edmund or indeed of myself. But since you ask me now, no, Susan, I do not. We never speak of her.' She thought to herself that she tried never to think of her cousin, but there were times when Maria's guilt and misery would rise up as vivid presences in her mind.

'It is so very strange to think I have never met my cousin. And I think you never like to talk of her.'

'No, Susan. You know it was a very painful time, for us all.'

'Fanny, what would Maria do if Aunt Norris died?'

'Aunt Norris has always enjoyed good health. Let us hope she will continue vigorous and strong. What Maria did is too painful to contemplate. Once she seemed to me the child of good fortune, and now I know I am the fortunate one. I never thought I should come to live in Mansfield Parsonage, any more than we thought of you making your home in Mansfield Park. I cannot bear to think of Maria living in perpetual estrangement from this dear place, from her home and her parents. I never loved Maria and Julia as I love you, Susan dear, but we passed much of our girlhood together and they were – they were never unkind to me.'

During her girlhood, Maria had shown no sign of any attachment to Mansfield, but Fanny's own deep-rooted love of the place, the great house, her little white attic and her own dear east sitting-room, the green shrubberies, the grounds and gardens, the village, and the Parsonage, now her own home, where she lived so contentedly and busily with her beloved husband and young children, had made her think even more sorrowfully and compassionately of her cousin than when she had first heard the shocking intelligence of Maria's elopement with Henry Crawford, Fanny's own suitor. It was the more difficult for her to reflect on the episode because without it her own life must have been very different. Had Maria never left her husband for Henry, Edmund might never have discovered the grave discrepancy of feeling and morality which made Mary Crawford an impossible match for him, and turned to her, Fanny, first as sympathetic and affectionate cousin, then as dear friend, and in the end as beloved wife. Edmund might never have been her husband

and the father of the two children asleep in their beds upstairs, dear dear Edmund, whom she had loved since she first came to Mansfield Park as a child, to be daunted by the great rooms, long corridors and precious objects, to be rescued by her kind cousin from anxious fears, to be reassured, protected and taught.

When now and then she looked back at the unhappy past that had shaped her happy present, Fanny Bertram never cared to think that Edmund and Mary might have married, never consciously entertained the possibility that in time – without Edmund's love – she herself might have learnt to love Henry Crawford. When Maria's exile came unbidden into her memory and her imagination, it was sometimes followed by the memory of Henry Crawford, smiling at her, Fanny, speaking to her of his faithful love. There had been rare unbidden moments when she felt the shadow – it was a black shadow – of the never-to-be but might-have-been end of such love. When memory – lively, dangerous, memory – summoned these images, she could usually banish them by forcing her attention back to the everyday duties, in the here and now. But there were times – in the middle of the night, it might be, as she lay awake beside her sleeping husband after one of the children had cried and called her – when she could not find it easy to exercise such control. She felt certain that Edmund never looked back in sadness at his love for Mary. That love had died and had long since been buried, and Fanny knew her husband well enough to be certain that he never revisited its grave, that his affection was wholly and entirely hers. But her own more intense, susceptible and wayward fancy was not easily governed. And this evening, though she was wide awake, she found herself shivering, and the shadows in the room seemed to come closer.

'Are you cold, Fanny? Shall I put more wood on the fire? Is there a draught from the large window? Shall I get you a shawl?'

'No, no, thank you, it's nothing. I am sorry, it is only that we have been talking too long on too painful a subject, Susan. Let us think of something else. Let us talk of something else.'

But the sisters could not immediately hit on another subject of conversation, and each sank into her own thoughts. Susan thought of asking Fanny about her memories of the big house and the parsonage, when she had come from Portsmouth to Mansfield Park as a little girl of nine, to be cared for by her aunt and uncle in the great house, but something held her back from broaching this subject. Fanny had sometimes talked about these early days, but preferred to dwell on happier and more recent times, when she had grown closer to her aunt and uncle, as a beloved daughter with a life of her own, not as a dependent. One subject Susan knew she must never bring up – that of Henry Crawford, the wealthy and dashing young man who had eloped with Maria Rushworth, their married cousin, Henry, who had paid court to Fanny, and whom she herself had met when he had paid a flying visit to Portsmouth. She had listened and looked with sharp-eyed interest as she walked along the sea-front with Fanny and her handsome visitor.

As she looked into the fire, Fanny's memory was travelling even farther back: she was remembering her very first acquaintance with the parsonage. When she had first come to live at Mansfield, her uncle Mr Norris, though elderly and ailing, was the incumbent, and when she came to the parsonage, she was never welcomed as a guest but employed by her aunt Norris, always given tasks to perform inside and outside the house, mending sheets, sewing shirts, running errands, weeding flower-beds, picking herbs. Small for her age, never strong and given to the backache and the headache, kept down by her unloving, cross and critical aunt, she had been used to associate the house with fatigue and oppression. Later, when the pleasant and hospitable Grants had moved in, she had been there once or twice, but did not call at the house as a frequent visitor until she was much older, and even then, when she was made most welcome by Mrs Grant and Mary Crawford, she had felt some awkwardness, first because of Edmund's feeling for Mary Crawford, later because of Henry Crawford's feeling for her. Of Henry and Mary she would never willingly speak to anyone. It was a long time since she had spoken of the brother and sister to her husband, who had once wanted her to marry Henry, and who had once hoped to marry Mary. She did not like to think of all that. She gave herself a little shake.

As Fanny looked about her, she saw amongst the common possessions, hers and her husband's, her old books, and some of her old pictures, the childish drawing of HMS Victory that William had drawn and that had once hung in the east room, the old schoolroom, her nest of comforts. The large inlaid workbox by her side had been a present from her cousin Tom. The old beloved objects had been joined by others, some of Edmund's books, a large water-colour of Mansfield Park and a work-table with pleated green silk, presents from Sir Thomas and Lady Bertram.

She looked about her, and as she looked the scene changed, the familiar objects grew cloudy. She saw the parlour where she and her sister were sitting by the friendly fire, as it had once been before it became her own, recognisable but different, her treasures replaced by alien properties and possessions. The evening was warm but Fanny shivered in the quiet room that no longer seemed to be her own but was too full of shadows – flickering, shifting shadows, strange but familiar, not transparent but solid.

Two groups of people, young and old, were seated at separate tables. It was an evening party. It was the same room, her own drawing-room, but the lights and shadows fell with a difference. The candle-light fell on four middle-aged people playing a rubber of whist, intent and saying little, at a green baize card-table, and six other people, all young except for her aunt Bertram, playing a round game at a bigger table, laughing and joking and puzzling aloud as they speculated, tossed their cards on to the shining mahogany, prompted each other, lost and won. She was there herself as she had once been, young shy Fanny Price with her beloved sailor brother William who was home on leave, with her neighbours and close acquaintances, the lively Mary and Henry Crawford, her cousin Edmund, and her aunt, languid slow good-tempered Lady Bertram, who was being instructed in the rules of Speculation while her husband, the serious whist-player, enjoyed his whist without hindrance or distraction, with her aunt Mrs Norris and the Grants, that evening's host and hostess. She saw herself and felt herself as a ghost, in the past but in the present too, too vividly conscious of the past in what she knew was her parlour, her house.

She shook herself awake, from what had not been sleep, to shiver, to hold out her hands to the warmth, to feel and look at the gold wedding ring on her hand, to see Susan sitting on the black sofa, gazing into the red fire. Back in the world of ordinary things, in the present, in her own parlour, in her own house. The all too solid ghosts had gone, once more become mere memories. That was all they were. Sometimes they could be shut out, but not always. Henry and Mary were not dead but leading their lives somewhere in England, happy or unhappy, perhaps sometimes thinking of Fanny and Edmund Bertram.

The big round mahogany table and the small card table at which they had sat and played Speculation and whist, the sofa, the chairs, the golden elegant harp, the paintings and ornaments which had looked so solid and substantial, were gone, long gone, taken away, removed to other houses, sold, given away, bequeathed, fallen into disrepair. The people too were all gone away. The food-loving and hospitable Rector was dead and buried; his friendly, patient, discreet wife Mrs Grant, who had planted the shrubbery still flourishing outside the window, and the gravel path on which Fanny walked every day, was a widow living somewhere in London. Fanny's own brother William was a Commander in the Navy, on the *Endymion* in the Mediterranean; her beloved husband was visiting a sick parishioner eight miles away in Thornton Lacey; the clever, witty and beautiful Mary Crawford who had once played the harp for Fanny and Edmund by the large window, and her brother Henry Crawford, who had taught Fanny and her aunt to play at Speculation, courted Fanny, and then one day eloped with her married cousin Maria, – these who were once her close companions, who knew where they were now, or with whom? They were part of her life, in the past, and now and then in the present. The Crawford brother and sister were never mentioned nowadays in Mansfield Park or Mansfield Parsonage, where they had visited and stayed, which had once been so important to them, and where they had once been so important, to the Grants, to the Bertrams, and to Fanny Price. They might be happy again. Henry would have not suffered exile and humiliation like the unhappy Maria. She put that thought away from her. She was glad she did not know where he and his sister were.

'Fanny, shall I ring for the candles?'

'No, Susan, please not. Let us stay in the fire-light a little longer.' She gave herself another shake. 'I must stop this brooding. Our talk has been bringing me gloomy thoughts and I have been dreaming of the past. Memory is a gift to be cherished, as I have often thought, but it can hurt and pierce. I must remember that I have no occasion to feel sad. I know I am most fortunate, and most happy. I am so happy for you too, dear Susan. I know that you are busy and content with Aunt and Uncle at Mansfield Park, and have grown very dear to them both. Indeed, you are closer to our uncle than I have ever been, kind and affectionate though he has always been to me.'

Then she added, 'And I hope and trust that one day you too will enjoy such deep home-happiness and content as mine.'

Susan sat upright in her corner of the sofa. 'Fanny, I do not comprehend you. What can you mean? Can you be speaking of marriage? Of my marrying? You are, are not you?' In the dim light Susan looked hard at her sister, who had spoken rapidly and most earnestly. Fanny did not reply. Susan persisted, her voice becoming agitated. 'I thought I could rely on you at least not to make matches, like the rest of the world.' She gave a little laugh. 'Well, in truth, not everyone else. Aunt Bertram may be relied on not to contemplate my marrying. The other day she was saying how happy she was that I should never leave Mansfield Park, and my uncle smiled, and said he hoped some day to see me in a house of my own, as he was happy to see you. I did not know what to say, but replied I was most happy as I was.'

'And what did my aunt say?'

'Nothing at all; I think she had fallen back into her sofa and her after-dinner doze. But truly, Fanny, I am surprised at this. I did not expect you to raise the subject of my marriage. I confess I wish you had not. Of course I delight to see you and your husband and children, such good examples of married love and family life, but I am not of the opinion that all marriages are good, nor indeed that an unmarried woman cannot lead an active and a fulfilled life.'

'Susan, I meant no harm. I was thoughtless. I ask your pardon. I was not thinking. I was not thinking of marriage or of your future. I was thinking of something else. The words came to my lips, unpremeditatedly. I do not know where they came from. I am very sorry. I was not thinking of you, my dear, only of myself. It must be the twilight and talking of the past that has brought back memories that made feel happy at first but then sad, perhaps a little morbid. Suddenly the room seemed full of shadows, and I was trying to banish them, I suppose. I was trying to put aside the sadness and feel grateful for all my blessings. No, indeed, I am the very last woman to suppose that marriage must be every woman's aim and end, even though it has brought me great joy. I myself once suffered from all the world supposing that I would accept a charming, rich young man just because he was charming, rich and young – in other words, a good match. As you know. And of course I know that there are many women who lead useful and contented lives without being married and having children.'

'And many others who lead useless and most miserable lives being married, like Maria. And Julia, married to that addle-pated Yates. She did not seem in the seventh heaven of bliss when they last visited Mansfield Park. She spoke to him impatiently, and only laughed when he was not there.'

Fanny shook her head and said nothing. Susan paused, then resumed her subject, her voice rising. 'Mr Norris cannot have enjoyed much happiness with our stingy, greedy, cross-grained aunt. I am afraid that even my uncle seems happiest when he is writing, or playing whist, or talking with you and Edmund, or his steward, or looking at the newspaper after dinner when aunt is fallen asleep.'

Fanny and Edmund, who shared their deepest feelings, had observed Sir Thomas's delight in their growing family, and knew that it must in some measure console him for his disappointment in his own daughters, though he and Edmund had not spoken for several years of the hasty marriage of Julia and the disastrous fate of Maria. Fanny knew that Sir Thomas rejoiced in the close friendship and sisterly love of Susan and Fanny, but she had reflected also that the new family affections must be sources of regret to him as well as joy. Her fondness for her uncle, like most human feeling, was finely chequered, mingling gratitude with pity, esteem with regret, wonder at his misplaced trust in Mrs Norris, and sympathy for what she knew must be self-reproach.

'Susan, you speak too vehemently. Of course you are right, in what you say about Maria and Aunt Norris, and perhaps about Julia too – though I hope things are not too unhappy for her – but please not to talk so about Uncle and Aunt Bertram. It is better not to say such things. They hurt me very much. And it is not right – it is not respectful to talk so. Aunt and Uncle have been very good to us. To me first, taking me into their family when I was very young, and then later to you. They have given us both shelter, occupation, a home, and love. They provided for us in ways that our own parents could not.'

'I am sorry, Fanny. All you say is true. I was speaking vehemently, as you say – hastily – carelessly – thoughtlessly – as you know I am wont to do. But I spoke from my experience. I have not even mentioned our own parents, and our own home. I believe you and Edmund provide the only example of a good marriage I have ever known. When I spoke like that about the bad examples, including those at Mansfield Park – oh, you know my impetuous downright way which startled you when we first met in Portsmouth – it was because I want you to know that I shall never be like Maria, or Julia. If I cannot be like you and be fortunate enough to find a husband I can esteem as well as love, and who will esteem and love me, I shall be content to stay plain Susan Price, a rational, useful and busy woman, so therefore a happy one, to the end of the story. And please to remember that I love my nieces and nephews, your children, William's little ones. And Tom will not stay single for ever; he must settle some day, as Aunt is always saying, as I am sure Uncle wishes. I can relish the pleasures of being an aunt. I think they will not grow less as I grow older. I do not need to marry.'

Fanny got up from her chair and embraced her sister, saying, 'Dear Susan, I am the one in fault, for speaking – or seeming to speak – about your marrying. I love and esteem what you call your downright way, so different from my own timidity and shyness. I value your fearlessness and openness. Because of them you can help

Aunt and Uncle so much better than I ever did. I was always too timid, too shy, a creepmouse as dear Tom once called me. That word hurt me a little, but he was right. And I can trust that you will never throw away your affections, because I know you to be rational indeed, as you say, as well as affectionate. But I think that we have talked enough – too much – about ourselves. I am sorry to have offended you. Tonight was to have been a restful time for you – a release from undoing the endless mistakes in my aunt's needlework, to do nothing but be my guest and take your ease on the sofa.'

Susan laughed, and sank back again on her cushions. 'It has been rest indeed, and a delight to talk like this. But shall we not return to another of our old Portsmouth habits, and read something aloud? That would not be too onerous for me, you know, but a refreshment. I will not venture to suggest Mrs Radcliffe, especially in this dim light, and I think you do not care for her, but perhaps your favourite Crabbe?'

'Mr Crabbe. What a good thought, Susan. Would you like to read me something of his last volume? It is on the small bookshelf over there, and though it is poetry, it will satisfy your love of a good story, and it will bring me down to earth, and common sense, which I need tonight. We have an hour before the carriage will come for you, and it is time I called for lights and took up my work. Edmund's new shirt-cuffs will never be finished if I go on saying whatever comes into my head, or foolishly dreaming in this half-light.'

She stood up, shivered again, gave herself a shake and laughed. 'Yes, we need lights now. I have been imagining all manner of things, here in the dusk, by the fire, with odd lights and shadows everywhere.

Note

Fanny Price is one of Jane Austen's most introspective and ruminative characters, and one who not only demonstrates but consciously praises the faculty of memory and the power of its emotional continuities. I have imagined the pain that involuntary memory, especially of her husband Edmund's former love for their old acquaintance Mary Crawford, must have caused her now and then, after she became Fanny Bertram and eventually went to live in Mansfield Parsonage, whose rooms and garden had witnessed some interesting scenes in her past. Such unwanted and disturbing memories would return in her private reflections only: she would not reveal them to her sister or her loving but less introspective husband.

Mrs Knightley's Invitation

Why she did not like Jane Fairfax might be a difficult question to answer; Mr Knightley had once told her it was because she saw in her the really accomplished young woman which she wanted to be thought herself; and though the accusation had been eagerly refuted at the time, there were moments of self-examination in which her conscience could not quite acquit her. But 'she could never get acquainted with her: she did not know how it was, but there was such coldness and indifference whether she pleased or not; and then, her aunt was such an eternal talker...' From Chapter 20 of *Emma* by Jane Austen

Mrs Knightley was concerned to see that Mrs Churchill looked fatigued, even paler than usual, with dark circles round her eyes. She was in deep mourning, wearing it now to mark three sudden deaths, which had followed each other in a quick succession, that of her husband Frank's uncle, Mr Churchill of Enscombe, then that of Mr Weston, her father-in-law, who had married Emma's beloved governess, and now that of her aunt, Miss Bates, who had died of heart failure a week before.

Jane spoke in subdued tones, 'It is very good of you to come, Mrs Knightley. As it was very good of Mr Knightley, to help me with advice, and with the funeral arrangements, since Frank could only ride over for the day. He was a great support and comfort to us both'.

'Of course Mr Knightley was so glad to be of any help, at such a sad time, and in my turn I want to do anything I can, as an old friend of your aunt and grandmother, of whom my own dear father has always been so fond.'

Emma coloured at her own words, remembering Mr Woodhouse's habitual solicitude and kindness towards Miss Bates and her mother in their impoverished days, before Jane's marriage, but also recalling with a sharp stab her own habitual intolerance of the garrulous aunt, and in particular the occasion at Box Hill when she had been unpardonably rude, in public, in the presence of Jane, to the well-meaning Miss Bates. It was an occasion she could never forget, not least because Mr Knightley – George – to whom she was now so happily married, had remonstrated with her afterwards, criticising her conduct severely, candidly, memorably. She made herself put aside that old painful memory and wondered what she might say now that would break the silence and be acceptable to Jane Churchill, with whom she had hardly ever felt at ease.

It was strange to stand there in the small parlour which she had never visited without enduring the dead aunt's vivacious outpourings, hard not to expect that foolish fond minuteness. When she had turned the corner of the steep staircase to the apartments on the upper floors, to pay her call, it had been strange not to hear Miss Bates's customary loud greeting coming from the landing above, 'So good of you … that is a sharp turn … I am sorry the staircase is so badly lit … dear Miss Woodhouse, do please take care' – but she must not mingle memory and mimicry in this way. Once she had not respected the living woman. Now she must respect the dead. She must proffer her help.

She had agreed with her husband and her father that she would call this morning to offer hospitality on behalf of the family. Mr Knightley, always respectful and solicitous for his father-in-law, under whose roof he was living, and at the present time more than usually tenderly concerned for his wife, who was expecting their first child in a few months time, consulted with them both about helping Jane Churchill and her old grandmother, and they had all three been of one mind. Emma was come to Jane Churchill bearing a sincere neighbourly invitation, but now she hesitated, anxious not to vex sad and sensitive feelings by seeming officious and pressing, carefully choosing her words before she spoke.

'Mr Knightley told me how exceedingly difficult – how very painful – it has been for you, with your little girl recovering from the croup, and poor Mrs Bates so very ill and so very shocked. I was very glad that Mr Knightley has been able to be of some assistance, but now we are most are anxious to do all that is in our power to help until your grandmother is quite recovered.'

'Mr Knightley has been most kind, as he always is. I do not know what I should have done without him this last terrible week. He will have told you that my husband – that Frank – could not come before the funeral, or stay with us afterwards, because we have no-one in the Richmond house with whom we could leave the child for long, only a new nurse and a very young and inexperienced nursemaid. We thought it necessary that Frank be away as little as possible. Elinor is only two. Grandmother is very shocked indeed, and keeps her bed. Of course we have long had anxieties about her because of her age, but we did not dream that Aunt Hetty might be taken from us. When we moved down from Yorkshire to

Richmond – it was only two months ago – it was with such happy expectations of being able to help my aunt with grandmother and see them both more often, even persuade them to come to us. The death of Frank's father was so sudden, and then to be followed so quickly by my aunt's – it was all so very shocking. My grandmother was badly shaken. I had hoped the shock would wear off but it shows no signs of doing so, and as Mr Knightley may have told you, Mr Perry fears her heart may be affected. He has hopes of her recovery but thinks it may be some time before she can travel, so there was no question of my taking her home immediately after the funeral, as Frank and I had first hoped. And as you know better than anyone, Mrs Knightley, because Mrs Weston is shortly to be confined, she is in no position to help anyone but herself and little Emma, and still suffering from her sad bereavement. She has always been so kind to me and Frank, and now she is so distressed for me, with grandmother so ill. Doubly distressed because she knows we cannot turn to her, herself deeply shocked and needing help.'

'Mrs Weston has been exceedingly brave since Mr Weston's death – it was so very sudden and distressing for her but also for your husband, after losing his other father – Mr Churchill. And now your aunt. So very distressing. So many deaths all in a huddle. But please, Mrs Churchill – Jane – I beg you will not stand on ceremony: do not call me Mrs Knightley, let us be Emma and Jane. I know that you and I have never been close friends, but please do not let our lack of friendship in the past stand in the way of my helping you now. Once – it was a little while before we were both married – I remember saying to you that I felt I was beginning to know you.'

Emma warmed to the memory, but she thought Jane's responding smile forced and artificial, as she replied, 'Yes, I recollect the occasion very well.'

'I have very much regretted that circumstances have prevented our coming to know more of each other: Mr Knightley and I hoped that we should meet more frequently after your move to Richmond …'

Even as she was speaking, as warmly and sympathetically as she could, she felt a return of the habitual ceremony, even coldness, that had always marked their relation. Perhaps on that memorable occasion when they had bidden each other farewell, each newly and happily betrothed, loved, loving, released from anxiety, and looking forward to a happy union, their flow of sympathy and goodwill had reached its highwater mark. Soon afterwards Jane had married Frank Churchill, and they removed to Enscombe in Yorkshire, remaining there until the death of Frank's uncle made possible their recent removal to Richmond, within easy distance of Jane's aunt and grandmother. There had not yet been time for any resumption of the old acquaintance, and now Emma and Jane were speaking with extreme politeness and formality, almost as strangers.

Emma went on, 'Please to forgive me for taking the liberty as an old friend and neighbour, but I know this house is too cramped for you to be comfortable, too small for any friend to move in and give you the help you need. I do not want to be importunate but – pray pardon me – I know that you have only one good bedroom and a closet here. Do please come to us, to Hartfield. I beg you. When Mr Perry told him your grandmother should not travel for at least two weeks, Mr Knightley consulted with me and my father, who is an old friend of your grandmother's and – as you will know – always particularly sympathetic to neighbours in times of illness.'

'Of course you are right, Mrs Knightley, these rooms are few, small, pitifully inconvenient. I know Mr Woodhouse has always been a kind friend to my aunt and grandmother, but I could not think of burdening him. I know his health has never been good.'

'My father's health is no worse than it has been for several years, I assure you. We are all most eager to receive you at Hartfield. It would be a kindness to us, if you come. My father is shocked and distressed by your aunt's death, as are we all, as Mr Knightley will have told you.'

Emma paused, at the thought of Miss Bates, dead and buried. It was hard to think of that tongue now stilled, harder still to think of her own neglect, and even worse, her unkindness. But she must not think of the past, but the present. She must resume, must persist, must urge her invitation.

'Perhaps you will believe how very well my father is when I tell you that he is strong enough in body and mind to have agreed to move with us to Donwell Abbey at the end of the year. We had not been sanguine about persuading him, but at last we succeeded. Hartfield is not as large as Donwell but it is a capacious house, as you know, and Father's old well-tried servants have known Mrs Bates for as many years as they have been with us. She and your aunt came to spend the evening with my father two weeks ago when Mr Knightley and I were engaged with Mrs Weston, and they were kind enough to keep him company. You will be able to engage a nurse for Mrs Bates, until she is improved enough to go back with you – I know you cannot accommodate one here. Please do us the very great kindness of letting us help you both in this small way. Of course you will consult Mr Perry but Mr Knightley thinks he will agree that the short ride in the carriage can do her no harm, and once she is at Hartfield, there will be as much help as you both need until she is well enough to travel home with you.'

She held out her hands, and it was Jane Churchill's turn to colour. The two young women looked at each other in silence, each finding herself at a loss for words.

Jane Churchill and Emma Knightley were both handsome, clever, rich, and not long married, one to a young husband a little her inferior in good sense and feeling, the other to an older husband a little her superior in good sense and feeling. Perhaps because they had been recommended to each other from childhood as congenial companions, by the well-meaning and well-wishing inhabitants of Highbury, the two young women had never become close friends, never been more than polite acquaintances. Their circumstances, too, had put a gulf between them. Jane was an orphan who had been forced to work at improving her talents of mind and music, always having to anticipate supporting herself, intending to earn her living as a governess, while Emma was the beloved younger daughter of the elderly and valetudinarian Mr Woodhouse, flattered and indulged, disinclined for books and pianoforte practice, sensible always of the other young woman's superior zeal and accomplishment.

Emma had sincerely rejoiced in Jane's marriage to Frank Churchill, and on the last occasion they had been alone together they had enjoyed a conversation which had been intimate and confidential, though Emma might not have seen her old acquaintance depart from Highbury with unmixed regret. But in the present sad

circumstances she had needed no urging from her husband to
hasten to Mrs Churchill, afflicted by her aunt's sudden death, and
the collapse of her old and ailing grandmother, and surely in need
of a woman friend's support and sympathy.

On her side, Jane had been happy to receive the advice and
practical help of Mr Knightley, whose tactful friendship she had
long valued, but now she found herself less at ease with Emma,
whose light-hearted but public and indiscreet flirtation with Frank,
during her own clandestine engagement to him, while never causing
any long-lasting apprehension, had once brought her some vexation
and anxiety, short-lived, but painful, and not soon forgotten. Jane
and Emma had each felt, though never acknowledged, that they
were easier apart, hearing of each other's happiness and well-being
from their affectionate friends, the well-meaning loquacious Miss
Bates and the amiable discreet Mrs Weston. As they faced each now
other in the small parlour, the bright sun showing the pattern in the
worn carpet which Jane's aunt and grandmother had treasured as a
sacred relic, refusing Jane's offers of a handsome new one as they
had refused offers of new and larger accommodations, each lady,
outwardly self-possessed, was embarrassed by an old constraint.

Emma made herself smile, 'Come, please, Mrs Churchill, I beg
you to be generous and admit that you are unable to help your
grandmother as you wish, if you insist on remaining here. Should
Mrs Bates's recovery take a longer time than Mr Perry anticipates,
your husband and the little girl could both join you at Hartfield,
where you know my sister Isabella's children are often visiting.
Hartfield is accustomed to invalids, children and nursemaids. You
must miss your daughter very much.'

Jane's eyes filled with tears. She seemed about to speak, but said nothing.

'Do please accept the hospitality – the very willing hospitality – of old friends. Pray do not look coldly on this invitation. Your acceptance will give us very great pleasure. It will relieve Mrs Weston's anxieties also. I saw her yesterday – I drive to Randalls every day – and she is so troubled at being unable to help, as of course you understand.'

Jane was relieved to turn the subject, 'Most certainly. I have received her messages, and letters, and sent her a note – I could not write at length – by Mr Knightley. He has been a most kind friend, as he always has been to me and my aunt and grandmother.'

Emma smiled but there was nothing for her to say in reply to Jane's praise and appreciation. The subject of Mrs Weston was exhausted and brought a new silence. Then both ladies began to speak at once.

'Can I not persuade you …?'

'Mrs Knightley, I am afraid …'

Emma gave way, and Jane went on, speaking slowly and hesitantly.

'I am sorry to appear ungrateful – unwilling to accept such very kind offers, but I am unable – I cannot think of it – on no account could we all come to Hartfield. Of course you are right, I feel most distressed at having to be away from Elinor. Until yesterday I could not think what to do. But I have been talking the matter over with Mr Perry – who as you well know, has been my aunt's friend and kind adviser for many years, and who knows us all well. He has known me since I was a child, and last night he came – after his daily visit – to propose that a nurse whom he has frequently employed in such cases, a superior and experienced woman, can come to us until grandmother is better. He did not think of her before, because she was occupied with another case, but now finds her patient recovered, so she is free to come to us. Yes – these rooms are few, and very cramped, but the nurse who is recommended, a Mrs Brown, a widow, will sleep anywhere – on a mattress on the floor – being accustomed to sickroom hardships. And as soon as grandmother is able to travel, which we hope may be before very long, Frank will come in our carriage – it is most commodious – and the nurse can return to Richmond with us all. I am most happy to have the prospect of such support until grandmother is quite recovered. I am most grateful, please believe me, Mrs Knightley, for your very kind offers of hospitality, but such an imposition is quite out of the question, and in the event, you will agree, not necessary.'

'I think you did not mention this idea to my husband?' Emma felt surprise and some little hurt. Mr Knightley had been so certain that the proposal of Hartfield hospitality would be acceptable to Mrs Churchill.

'I did not entertain the possibility until after Mr Knightley left me yesterday, when Mr Perry came in the evening and told me of the nurse, who was leaving her last case, a elderly patient of his whom he had been visiting. I had been too distracted to think and make plans, and am so grateful that he hit on this convenient solution. You have been most sympathetic, Mrs Knightley, and I thank you – all of you, you, Mr Knightley and Mr Woodhouse – for your kind – your more than kind offer of hospitality.'

Jane held out her hand, in a gesture of grateful decision. She had been visibly shaken and distressed, especially when talking of the little girl, but now she appeared resolute. There could be no more talk on the subject. Emma saw that Jane's calmer speech and warmer smile signified the end of a difficult conversation. She knew that when she was returned home, and told the story to her husband, without making mention of her disappointment and chagrin, Mr Knightley would take her by the hand, shake his head, smile, say nothing, and understand. Nothing more would be said by either of them on the subject, and her father would quickly become engrossed in hearing the details of Mr Perry's scheme, the illness and convalescence of his elderly patient, and the timely appearance of the experienced nurse, Mrs Brown, the widow.

She shook hands, speaking her last words of sympathetic and reluctant acquiescence as Jane showed her to the stairway, 'I am very sorry you will not come to us. Mr Knightley and my father will be disappointed but of course you know best. Please to let us know if there is anything you need, in the way of assistance or supplies, while you remain in Highbury.'

Mortified by regret and self-reproach, Emma was also relieved as she made her careful way down the narrow stairway she had so often ascended and descended when paying her dutiful calls, to the accompaniment of kindly warnings and grateful welcomes from Miss Bates, whose well-meaning talkative ghost must now and then trouble the quiet of Emma's conscience.

Note

At the end of their novel Emma Woodhouse and Jane Fairfax part on friendly terms, but we may reflect a little on their future acquaintance: Mr Weston is Frank Churchill's father and Jane's father-in-law, and Mrs Weston was Emma's governess and is her good friend, so Jane and Emma would inevitably have met in Highbury, but it is hard to imagine them becoming close friends. I have ventured to kill off Miss Bates and create a meeting which tests what Charles Lamb would have called the 'imperfect sympathies' of Mrs Knightley and Mrs Churchill.

Adèle Varens

'But unluckily the Varens ... had given me this filette (sic) Adèle; who she affirmed, was my daughter; and perhaps she may be, though I see no proofs of such grim paternity written in her countenance ... I acknowledged no natural claim on Adèle's part to be supported by me, for I am not her father; but hearing she was quite destitute, I e'en took the poor thing out of the slime and mud of Paris, and transplanted it here, to grow up clean in the wholesome soil of an English country garden.' From Chapter 15 of *Jane Eyre* by Charlotte Brontë

You have not quite forgotten little Adèle, have you, reader? I had not; I soon asked and obtained leave of Mr Rochester to go and see her at the school where he had placed her. Her frantic joy at beholding me again moved me much. She looked pale and thin: she said she was not happy. I found the rules of the establishment were too strict, its course of study too severe for a child of her age: I took her home with me. I meant to become her governess once more; but I soon found this impracticable; my time and cares were now required by another – my husband needed them all. So I sought out a school conducted on a more indulgent system; and near enough to permit of my visiting her often, and bringing her home sometimes. From Chapter 38 of *Jane Eyre*

i

Before the Visit

Neither Edward nor I ever spoke of rebuilding Thornfield Hall, which has remained a black ruin, never visited by us. After our marriage we decided to make our permanent home in Ferndean, the happy place of our reunited affections, where I had come when he called to me, when he wanted me and I most wanted him, when I was torn and distressed and had almost cast in my lot with my cousin St John Rivers, almost went with him to work as a missionary in India, for the sake of Christian labour and duty, but not for love. Across space, Edward Rochester's voice had summoned me, and I answered him and had come first to discover the ruin of Thornfield, then to Ferndean, which became my home, the home I had always longed for, our home, where our son was born and where Edward has begun to recover the sight of his remaining eye.

It is a healthier place now than it was when Edward sought refuge there after the burning of Thornfield and the death of his first wife, Bertha Rochester. Once he had thought it too damp and unsalubrious a place to hide the woman he had sequestered in Thornfield's attic, but now Ferndean's greenery is benign, its damp banished, its walls dried and whitened, its rooms no longer closely encircled by deep woodland. Before the birth of our first child, James Edward, we had a great swathe of the thick surrounding wood cut down, the site re-planted, the lake filled in, all the grounds cleared of trees, large shrubs and deadwood, and thoroughly drained. Old out-buildings, stables and barns were pulled down and a new conservatory built. We let in the sun. Bow windows replaced the small leaded lights, and the rooms were refurnished, ancient worm-eaten panelling stripped, walls re-painted in light colours and rotting fabrics replaced by flowered chintzes and pale linens. James was provided with a large bright nursery and modern furniture. As Edward's sight began to improve he could see not only his son's black eyes, exactly like his own, but the daylight streaming through shining glass, and outside in the garden all the old-fashioned plants that used to grow in the gardens of Thornfield, blooming in parterres and flower-beds round the new-turfed lawns – rose, jasmine, carnation, lavender, stock and southernwood. We planted one corner of Ferndean with plum, apple and cherry, in memory of the old orchard in Thornfield, where we had sat together and talked, as master and governess, as friends, and at last as affianced lovers.

'Adèle will be delighted by the bright rooms and the garden full of flowers. And by Jamie, of course', I said as I poured Edward's coffee early one June morning.

'Jane, you have planted the summer flowers in my garden and in my heart, but I do not know why you wish to disturb our precious solitude *à deux* by always bringing that brat here.'

'Edward, it is no longer a solitude *à deux*. We are a family now. Adèle is not a brat. I know very well that when she was eight or nine, when I first came to Thornfield, she was vain and spoilt and frivolous, but you know that there was very good reason for it. And she is much changed. Please to give me credit for some improving and steadying influence. Oh Edward – you are wearing your fierce look. She will only be here for a week or two. I have no desire to interrupt her studies but Miss Dalrymple writes that she is doing well, and will lose nothing by a brief holiday. And how can you say I bring her always? I have always visited her more often than she comes here, but as you know very well I have been unable to do that for the last months. Now I want Adèle to share a little of our new happiness, and meet her brother.'

'Her brother! How can you call James her brother! Stuff! That is just like you, Jane, to talk nonsense and fantasy. You never were like an ordinary mortal: your feet may be on the ground but your head is in the clouds. I want some peace and quiet now that dragon of a nurse has gone. I want to enjoy my wife and my son and my new garden full of the scent of flowers and a sunlight I can feel on my face, and begin to see.'

'Edward, do not rage so. I will not agree to shut Adèle off from a family life she has never known. The life I never knew in my childhood. To set her outside our home and warmth, to think of her outside our family circle, would be to cast a chill black shadow on it.'

'And you can pronounce the word brother! Can you call her James's sister?'

'Yes indeed I can, and I dare to hope that you can too. Look in your heart. Remember that you once called me "*sa petite maman anglaise*". How could you make a hideous difference between them?'

'Because there is a difference. A great difference. Whan I called you Adèle's "*maman*", you were not my child's real mother. James is our child. He is the flesh of my flesh, the bone of my bone.'

'Edward Fairfax Rochester, it is your fault and not your triumph, that you cannot say the same of Adèle, that you cannot look at her with the same pride and certain knowledge.'

'Very well, Jane, those words pierce and sting, but go on, go on. I should be able to bear it. I can bear it. Speak out, hard, plain and strong, as you always have spoken to me since that evening long ago when you told me I was not handsome and no philanthropist.

You are the one human being I know who does not flatter and does not lie. Go on.'

'I think I have said all I can say. Edward, please. Let her come.'

'Very well. Do as you like about the girl's visit.'

'And you will welcome her … be kind to her?'

'Was I ever unkind to her?'

'You sent her away to that strict narrow school.'

'Yes, very well, I sent her away, but what else could I do? That was after you left Thornfield, and I was alone, in that terrible house; I was in no mind to ask advice from friends and neighbours about schools for girls, was I? What friends and neighbours had I then? You were gone, and your whereabouts were unknown. And later on, after the fire, I could scarcely send for her then, could I? After I had lost my sight and the use of my left hand. When I was in an agony of spirit that almost numbed the agony of my body.'

'Dear Edward, I understand all that, of course I do, but do you not understand that her time at the school was very difficult for her, who had been so much indulged? I had left her, as well as you. I can never forget how sad and thin she was when I went to see her there. How she smiled and cried with joy to see me again. When I brought her home then, please to remember that it was only for a month or so. I had to agree that it was too difficult for me to care for you as I wished, and as you needed, and also teach and care for her, and once more we sent her away. She is happier at Miss Dalrymple's school but now because of Jamie I have not seen her for several months. That is cruel for her. Now your sight is coming back, you can see your child, you are not in agony of body or spirit, and you need my physical help and support much less.

Dear, I shall always be by your side. We have so much, and she has nothing. Our house is in order, the monthly nurse is gone. So do please welcome Adèle. I am not asking for her to stay here always. But remember that she is still a child. Remember that you were kind to her when her mother abandoned her. Remember how you prayed, after you and I were separated, and how your prayers were answered. Shall I show you the passage where Christ rebuked his disciples for pushing aside the little children?'

I got up and went to the high reading-desk with the great family bible on it, which we had moved into the dining-room when we rearranged the house, moving furniture to make space for Edward to walk, first assisted by me, then alone, as his sight began to improve.

He laughed. 'No need for that. I may have been a bad Christian but I went to church as a boy; I have a good memory and as you know, I have come to trust God and be thankful for all my mercies. Ah, Jane! Very well. I am subdued. When does your little French girl come?'

'Our little French girl. She grows less French and more English with the years: though if she is still French, and if that is a fault in your eyes, it is your fault and not hers, is it not?'

'That is another harsh saying. No more. I thank you for that smile. How can I refuse you anything, my hazel-eyed Janet?'

'You know very well that my eyes are green. I will send for her next Monday, if you please.'

'Very well. Now I deserve a reward. Come and kiss me, Jane.'

ii

After the Visit

The carriage had taken our little English girl back to school, after she had spent her three weeks at Ferndean, helping me and the young nursemaid dress and undress little James, playing with him, talking baby nonsense to him, dancing him, weeding the flowerbeds, reading with me, and accompanying Edward's singing as I – whom he once dubbed 'a bungler' at the piano – could not do. It was high summer, and we were alone again, husband, wife and baby, with our old servants from Thornfield, John and Anna, and the man and woman who helped them.

I was sewing in the drawing-room after dinner, while Edward sat playing to me.

'Have you had enough one-handed music, Jane?'

'I love to hear you play, Sir, as well you know.'

'And I love you to call me "Sir" in that way, fond and playful, reminding me of our early days when you were the demure and respectful governess and you had no idea that I was falling under your spell, that deep enchantment.'

'I like to remember those days, too, as well you know. Let us remember together now. That was a sprightly and joyful piece you just played but now I should like us to talk together quietly. Please to come and sit here beside me.'

I put down my work on a side-table, gave him my chair, and sat down on a low stool, leaning back against his knee. In my bosom I wore a red rose-bud he picked for me that morning, as we strolled round the garden after putting Adèle in the carriage and waving goodbye. After he gave me my rose I had snapped off a sprig of southernwood, sniffed its odd fragrance and put it in his button-hole.

'There, a pungent herb for you, Sir.'

'Ah, Old Man for an elderly spouse! A grey leaf, also.'

'Not at all. Lad's Love for a youthful husband. And the shrub with many names is not grey but silver-green. Dear Edward, you look relaxed and happy.'

As I sat with him in the lamplight, my buried trouble stirred and could not be quietened. 'Edward, why are you glad about Adèle's departure? So very glad?'

After a silence he put out a hand to stroke my hair. 'I am sorry to offend you, Jane. I am sorry *you* are not glad – glad that I am relaxed and happy. Glad? Yes, I am glad. Relieved by her departure. Pleased that I can stop pretending to be affectionate and welcoming.'

'So all this time you have been wishing her gone? And when she was so happy and so grateful and so loving. I am sorry. Surely you must admit that she is greatly improved, more serious, more helpful.'

'She is quieter, I admit. But the girl is too insipid for my taste. I love the wine of the burnet rose, the spice of the pink, the bitter-sweet of your southernwood or Old Man. I have grown expert in scents since I had my time of blindness. Adèle reminds me of artificial scents. She is not a wild rose.'

'I am glad. I have no wish for a wild child.'

'Now you have tamed your wild lover?'

'Precisely, Sir. But seriously, I am truly grieved to think that you have been hiding your deepest feelings when I thought we were coming together, as a family of four.'

'Give me time, Jane, give me time. Please recollect that I have only recently become accustomed to being one of a family of three.'

He stroked my hair again, and turned my averted face towards him. 'Janet, I can keep nothing from you. You always tell me to look in my heart: let me try to tell you what I have found there. I shall not find it easy to say this, but since you press me, I must. You must understand that she – Adèle – is no flower but a thorn in my flesh, a reminder of her mother. My opera-mistress. And there is more. You told me before she came that I could never look on her with pride and delight as I look at James, my son, our son. No doubt you recollected that I denied my paternity, that I had told you I was sure she was not my child. That was a half-truth. You know better than anyone that I was a great dealer in half-truths, Jane. The whole truth is this: she may indeed be flesh of my flesh and bone of my bone, but I do not know; I cannot know; I will never know whether she is my child or not. I cannot be sure. I cannot see her clearly but when I hear her voice and laugh I hear Céline Varens and remember her small features and her light skin. I cannot see Adèle clearly, but as my sight improves I keep looking towards her and listening. Her presence is painful, at times a torture.'

'But Edward, it has not always been so – you have not always felt like this?'

'No, only since our child was born, and even more since I have seen – and heard – them side by side, seen and heard her playing with him, singing and babbling in English and French. Before that, even when I met you, and to meet you was to love you, and know you as my mate, even before I was free to make you mine, I could tolerate the girl. Even when you came back and found me maimed and blind, but free. Even after we were married, I could smile and tease her, be kind to her, give her dresses, recognise her mother's vanities in hers, take it all lightly, as I did at Thornfield. I knew that Céline was unfaithful to me, but as I told you long ago, my passion for her did not last long. But since I have looked at my child – our boy, who has my black eyes that you call brilliant, though God knows my sight is dimmed – everything has changed. I find it difficult to look at Adèle and I find it difficult to stop looking. My improving eyesight only torments me when I look at her. I dread the improvement which will bring you and Jamie, my treasures – but her also – more clearly into my view and vision. I fear to see more. I keep wondering whom she resembles. I keep wondering who her father was – not because I am jealous of her mother's infidelities but because I keep wondering if she might indeed be mine. I keep wondering if she should be called Adèle Rochester and not Adèle Varens. I keep wondering if I have any right to call James my firstborn, as he is yours. That is the most bitter thought. At times too bitter to endure, so I thrust it passionately away from me. Of course I rage. Of course I did not want her to come. Of course I am glad when she is out of my hearing, out of my sight – my recovering sight, for which I should be wholly grateful to God. Now you have heard the whole truth. You have heard unpalatable truths from me before. I think you prefer them to my lies. Jane, we were so happy after James was born, the three of us together, my sight returning and everything so easy. For the first time in my life, as it seemed. It is hard to lose that peace. It is hard to dread seeing better.'

'Edward, perhaps that ease was wrong, that peace too comfortable.'

'Jane, please to think what had gone before. I was blind and burnt; I had lost an eye; I had lost a hand; I was without you. I had no hope or dream of ever seeing you – of hearing your voice – again. Only Jane could deny me peace and comfort after such loss. You can be hard. I should know that by now.'

'Oh, Edward, I know you have suffered and I do not feel hard towards you, but I think it is better to face the truth – to see in Adèle what she is, and what she is not, to you. To live with the uncertainty. Even if it is hard. I know it is hard. I find it painful when you speak like this of your pain, of James being my first-born but perhaps not yours. What I called easy was your relaxed conscience. But I thank you for telling me the truth about your new feeling. I knew something was wrong, but I could not think precisely what it was. I too had not faced the thought – I had not truly thought of her as your daughter, but stupidly accepted what you first told me, though as I looked back, what you said was not very clear. I think you said, on that day in Thornfield long ago when you made your confessions – that Céline had told you she was yours but you saw nothing of yourself in her. I am sure you said – I can hear your voice as you said it –"I am not her father". But you cannot know that. At the time, since you had told me about her mother's infidelity to you, while she was under your protection, that all seemed reasonable, in its horrible way, and I did not question it. Now I have come to see – no, not see, but feel – that Adèle may be your child, and James's half-sister, by a woman you once cared for but came to despise. For you that possibility may be as painful to contemplate as ignorance – as not knowing and never knowing.'

'But will not that possibility – what you see as a possibility – change your own feeling for her – for the child? I know you are fond of her.'

'No, indeed, I am certain it will not. Do you remember asking me the same question when you first told me about her mother? it is the same answer now. It will make me love Adèle the more. Because I do love her. I am not jealous of her mother. I can never resent her. Remember that she is like me, a motherless child, and a child who never knew her father, but for some of her childhood, and unlike me in my childhood, she has not been quite unloved. However, unlike me, she will never know her true parentage. Long ago, when you talked to me about her history and your life with her mother I took her on my knee and caressed her, most fondly, as I had never been in the habit of doing. These past weeks while she was here I noticed that you seem to shrink from taking her hand or returning her kiss, but I do not and I never shall.'

'Jane, you are better and stronger than I am. To be honest – and my love for you is all honesty now – I do not think I can change my coldness into affection. It is a coldness. I feel that it should be fondness, Reason informs me that she may be my child, and that knowledge chills me to the bone. I love looking at you, and seeing you more clearly as the days pass. I can meet your honest look, my flinty-hearted Janet, as I met it when you told me you could not live with me, after you met my wife, in the Thornfield attic. Face to face. But yours is a look which can make me flinch.'

'Edward, be honest: have you come to regard the death of your first wife as the act of a kind and merciful Providence?'

'Janet, you forget that I tried to save her life.'

'I know. I shall never forget that. Perhaps I question you too harshly. Let me put it differently. We have come to think that our freedom to marry was a Providential gift. But perhaps my idea of Providence is not yours. My Providence is merciful but not gentle. I believe we are not allowed to escape entirely the shadow of our past life and actions. That would make Providence too soft in its forgiving. Providence does not bestow a happy ever-after, like an author of novels. It imposes hard discipline. You have ease and happiness, our marriage, our son, your partly restored sight, but Adèle presents you with a pain, a problem, a discord, a demand, not a healing, not a solution, not a harmony, not a gift. It is different for me; it is easier for me ...'

'It is, because I was the sinner and wanted you to sin, and you would not, and you have not been so severely punished.'

'No, indeed, certainly not for that reason. How could you think I meant that? No, Edward, because for me Adèle offers a benison and a duty. Her existence – her life with us – is in harmony with my past life; she is a child like my old self, and a child like my own child. Do you not understand? Perhaps it is easier for me because I am a woman. Perhaps it is easier too because I was her governess, who taught her and in teaching, cared for her, and watched her begin to grow up. I am so sorry, you look even more anxious and distressed now, but I had to know what was on your mind and tell you what was in mine. Edward, I have one more thing to say, and I say it most solemnly. You cannot be sure that our child is your first-born, and that thought pains me too but I thank God that he was born, whether first or second – though I wonder if that is because I am not weighed down by a man's pride, and a man's mistaken sense of honour? Think this: were it not for Adelè you and I would never have met, and James would have never been born.'

My voice sounded firm and confident but unshed tears burnt my eyes. I was glad of a long silence which I brought to an end by scrambling to my feet and saying, with a tremble in my voice, 'No, you need not say anything in reply. I do not want to say anything more tonight. We have had enough talk. It was painful for me as well as you. To be reminded of the unhappy things in the past. To think that you could find it painful, to see some things clearly, or more clearly. There are some things that can never come clear, in this life. I have charged you with not thinking enough about the past but there were some things I too did not understand. Forgive me for that blindness on my part, and Edward, put all this away for tonight. We cannot shut ourselves away from the past. Not entirely. You know that is true. But only think now that we are together and that our own dear boy is sleeping peacefully upstairs in his bed.'

He said nothing, and I ventured a little farther. 'Dear, if you are not too tired we might have more music. Some calm and peaceful chords, if you please. And thank you.'

My husband got up, stood still for a moment, looked toward me and nodded. I was not sure how clearly he could see my face, outside the small circle of amber lamplight, but I smiled to him and then to myself, as I watched him walk slowly down the long room, just touching the chairs and a table as he made his careful way to the piano.

Lucy and Paulina: the Conversation of Women

I liked her. It is not a declaration I have often made concerning my acquaintance in the course of this book: the reader will bear with it for once. Intimate intercourse, close inspection, disclosed in Paulina only what was delicate, intelligent, and sincere; therefore my regard for her lay deep.

....

Some lives *are* thus blessed … Other lives run from the first another course. Other travellers encounter weather fitful and gusty, wild, and variable – breast adverse winds, are belated and overtaken by the early closing winter night. From Chapter 32 of *Villette* by Charlotte Brontë

I had not seen Paulina Bretton for seven years or more, and as we met I observed that marriage and motherhood had bestowed on her a measured movement and a stately grace. She was still white-skinned and bright-eyed, and only a little more matronly in figure, but there was nothing in her gait and mien that recalled the diminutive old-fashioned child who shared my bedroom in Bretton or the piquante young lady I had encountered ten years later in Villette with her father. Nothing here of the effervescence, the darting playful charm, I reflected, as she walked slowly across the room towards me, her black heavy mantle, long black shawl and black bonnet too heavy and solemn for her small figure. Nothing here of the *pas de fée*. Her smile was grave but warm and there was no reserve in her eager embrace and kiss. As I gestured to a chair and sat down opposite her, the bright morning light showed horizontal lines on her brow and faint blue shadows under her large long-lashed eyes.

'My dear Paulina, I am glad to see you but very sad about the cause for your mourning. As I trust you know.'

'Dear Lucy, thank you with all my heart for the letter you wrote about Mary. You always write the good plain language of true friendship and that was a time when I badly needed it ... No fine phrases, no conventional formulae, but the plain simple words of sympathy, that you might have been uttering to us, face to face. I am so sorry you never saw her. I still find it hard to talk about her, so that is all I will say. I know you will understand. Graham sends you his warm regards and hopes to see you very soon, but this morning he has to see one of the professors at the Scientific Institute, and could not come with me. We hope you will be free to dine with us some evening this week. But I welcomed this chance to talk to you alone, as we have so often talked together in the past. Thank you for finding this space to see me in your busy day. Lucy, you have not changed. You are still Lucy Snowe.'

'I suppose I am. Paulina, I would have found a time for you at almost any hour, but as it happens this is the morning recreation time for the older girls. Yes, we have talked so often, have we not, you and I, over the years? Once in the early days when you almost broke your child's heart because Graham wouldn't let you come and play with his schoolfellows, and then again when your father finally took you away from my godmother's house where you had settled so happily.'

'And then again here in Villette when I thought he was in love with my cousin Ginevra – oh dear, poor Ginevra – and again when I told you that he had written to me and I had answered him and you advised me – dear Lucy, always so sensible and so good – not to keep the letters, and our affection, a secret from my father. So many times you gave me the best advice. I still remember some of the words you used. They were never commonplace, so not easily forgotten. You were … no, I will not say my conscience, that would be silly and perhaps blasphemous … but something like … the voice of Reason, that clear cool voice.'

As always she spoke quickly but every now and then paused to choose and weigh her words. Even after she had grown up she would occasionally lapse into her childhood's lisp, rousing her father's affectionate teasing, but her modulated speech had grown precise and firm, a scrupulous enunciation of thought.

'Dear me, that makes me sound dull and cold. The voice of Reason?'

'No, Lucy, not you – you were never dull or cold. My word was cool, not cold. Your voice was your own, unlike all other voices. You are smiling. I hope I am not growing pompous, though as a child I know I was inclined to be grandiloquent. I remember how I used to use big words I couldn't properly pronounce. I'll try again. Let me see. The voice of a reasoning heart, then. Is that better? But it was not only your words, it was your actions too. I knew you were tender-hearted when I was little, even though you always sounded so sensible and so controlled and so cool. I always remember how you took me into your bed when I couldn't get warm in my cold

little cot. I never forgot anything of that time. And here we are
again, after all the years, talking easily and honestly and freely as we
always did. Do you know, Lucy, you are the only real woman friend
I have ever had.'

She stopped, and for a moment neither of us said anything.

'Do not misunderstand me. I am perfectly happy in my marriage.
I love my husband and my children and I loved Grandmother
Bretton, who was my friend and steady support until she died.
She was a good mother-in-law to me as I know she was a good
godmother to you. Since we have settled in Windsor I have become
acquainted with my neighbours and the wives of Graham's friends
and colleagues. But I have had no intimate friend of my own, no-
one to whom I could talk as you and I talked when I was a child,
and later on when I was a young woman troubled by love. I am
blessed in my husband, and we talk together by the hour, not only
about our dear children but about his work and the newspapers
and the ways of the great world. But meeting you again like this
brings me straight away that old sense of quiet exchange. More
than that – it has given me a strange confidence, as if I could tell
you anything and everything.'

'Paulina, is there anything in particular you want to talk about
today?'

'No, Lucy, no. I did not come here this morning with any
particular subject in mind. I just want to talk. To let the words come
out, without forethought or constraint. I like the way you speak the
truth bluntly, and it encourages me to do the same. On my way here
I was feeling that we could say anything to each other – at least, that
I could say anything to you. I love that truthfulness, that ease, that

entire lack of social convention – oh, so different from the way people commonly talk to each other, the conversation of callers and mere acquaintances, talking polite nothings, passing the day, enquiring about health and children, other people's betrothals and marriages and deaths, and all the while caring nothing. You know what I mean. You do not lead an enclosed life. Your work here takes you into the world. I hear your pupils come from England and France and Germany as well as from Labassecour.'

'Yes, that is true. But I probably suffer less than you do from social forms, here in the school. I am fortunate in being able to plead my occupation and avoid mere callers. And avoid merely polite conversation. When I talk to the children, to my teachers, to parents, whoever they are and wherever they come from, there is almost always a real subject-matter, real questions and real answers. But I know what you mean and I too value our friendship, and feel as we talk now that it has not been weakened by our separated lives and the passing years.'

'Lucy, you have had your sorrows, I know. You have seen more of death than I, and from an early age, though you have not talked about it. In the past I could confide in you my love for Graham, and my anxiety for Papa, but you have never spoken to me of your family, your friendships, your plans for the future. You have always had your reserves, your silences, and your pride. I respect them, and during these last years when we have not met, perhaps I have grown to understand you better than I used to. I would not want to intrude now, but there are things we can talk about. Your life here in Villette, your success, this excellent school whose fame has reached your friends in England. Please to tell me you find satisfaction in your work. And you must take pleasure in this delightful and well-appointed house, a place of your own, your own treasured possessions.'

I followed her eyes as she looked round at the small parlour, its pink-flushed walls, polished wooden floor and square of dark-rose carpet, its piano, its bust of Beethoven, bookcases, china, fresh flowers, shining windows, and the garden where some of my pupils were taking their recreation. Yes, I valued my small household gods – the careful purchases and the beloved gifts – my gleaming chairs and tables, my growing plants, my own things and my own space inside and outside.

'The girls I passed,' Paulina went on, 'the little ones, and the big ones who are nearly women – when I came through the garden they all looked healthy and happy, and they were chattering and laughing under the trees and in the sun. I could hear someone practising scales through an open window. I remember Graham telling me about the dark *allée défendue* in Madame Beck's *pensionnat* but I am sure there is no *allée défendue* in your garden.'

'No, there is not. Of course the property is not extensive, even though I have fortunately been able to buy the house and garden next door, but what I have is a sunny green space with no dark walks or gloomy corners or nun's ghosts.'

As we smiled and talked I was also remembering Madame Beck's garden, the dark walk, the gloomy corners, and the old pear tree with a hollowed space where I had buried a sealed flask containing six letters, my letters from John Graham Bretton, Paulina Mary's husband, written to me in kind warm friendship before he had met her again and fallen in love with her. My buried letters – they were not love letters, but they were a little more than mere letters of friendship. They were letters which the writer had long forgotten, and letters which I no longer recalled with pain, letters which I would never disinter, letters which I had never mentioned even to Paul Emmanuel, whose letters to me were in an old lacquer box inside a locked cedar chest in my bedroom. They would be buried too, but buried with me.

'Yes, Paulina, I am content here. I like my house and my work and the people who work with me, teachers I can trust and pupils I can help. Growing children and girls. I have real work, useful and demanding, work that I am fitted to do. And in addition, I have books, music and fresh air whenever I need them for myself. I have what I find precious – time to myself. That is why I take only a very few boarders, and have mostly *externes*.'

'So you don't mind solitude?'

'Once I should have replied that I did not mind it, that I found it more tolerable than most company. But I have come to value and enjoy solitude. It brings me peace and quiet in the vacations, and at the end of each busy day, when I sit in the lamplight, and enjoy my reflections, and my memories. Not that I live in the past. The present and the future engage my thoughts also. I am a working woman.'

'Yes, of course you are. You know, Lucy, I find I do want to talk to you about something particular. It must have been at the back of my mind, where I was not aware of it until just now, when it came into the light, as thoughts do, with our talk and the bright morning. I did have a reason for my visit, after all, though I didn't see it until I saw the girls in the garden, your books and your music, and we began to talk.'

She got up and went to the piano. 'What have you been playing? Ah, Mozart.' She picked up one of the books on a side-table, 'Boz! Joyful music and amusing stories.'

'Dear Paulina, what did you expect? Confess now – Dido's lament and *Clarissa*?'

She blushed and laughed, 'Perhaps … but I am glad to be proved wrong.' She put down *The Pickwick Papers* and looked at another book which lay open beside it, 'Ah, I'm glad you still read Schiller – I must confess I have neglected my German. Do you remember our lessons with Fräulein Braun? You were much more tolerant of her than I was – I shrank from her enthusiasm and her insistent touching, and I hated having to kiss her cheek – but I loved studying with you – everything, from the hard grammar to the rapturous verses! You were such a conscientious student, but inspiring to me, not just a hard worker. Yes, they were good times, especially good for me because I had never had any disciplined schooling, thanks to my too indulgent papa who was always talking about sending me to school but who would never let me out of his sight! I love to remember those happy times. And of course I was learning to love Graham, all over again.'

She left the table and stood looking out of the window.

'I must tell you what just came into my mind. Lucy, do you remember once saying that Graham and I were the children of good fortune, destined to sail with propitious winds and temperate breezes. Others might be doomed to tempest and shipwreck …'

I shook my head, self-deprecating, but she went on, reading what was in my mind and perhaps on my countenance. 'Oh I know that you were not speaking in self-pity but long afterwards I remembered your words, and saw what they implied.'

'I remember I did think something like that but I do not recall saying it to you.'

'Well, you did, and your words were so vivid that they sank deep into my heart and remained with me. I do not want to complain, or lament my lot, but Graham and I have not always enjoyed sunshine and clement weather. As you know, we have lost a child, and there will always be that shadow on the happiness of our life. But that was not what I was going to say. A moment ago when I said you were my one real woman friend I felt an old pang – the pain at not remembering my mother. You may not remember that she and my papa were not happy, and she was one of those people who never grow up, who care for nothing but pleasure. In the end she died seeking pleasure. I think one of the reasons I disliked Ginevra was the thought that my own mother – another Ginevra, the first Ginevra – must have been like her.'

'Yes, I did know something of your mother, from my godmother, who told me about her death – and a little of her life – before you came to Bretton with your father.'

'I can scarcely remember my sorrow. I mean that sorrow I must have felt at her dying. It is no more than the memory of a memory. My father never spoke of her, but I knew much later – from Mrs Bretton, whom I questioned about my parents – that when she died he had been racked with guilt. I think that was why he left me with Mrs Bretton while he travelled. No, my sorrow was one which recurred throughout my girlhood and growing-up, and it was the sadness at not having a mother. I clung to my father, and then shared my love between him and Graham, but since I have had children and known what it was to love them and be loved by them, I have felt that loss of a mother more sharply, as something that can never be replaced. I do not tell you to ask for pity, but simply because I want to tell someone. It would hurt Graham if I told him – if I put it like that. He might think there was something I could not tell him. And something lacking in our life.'

'I understand.'

'Of course I do not often think of it. Only now and then. As I look around me and see other people's lives, I am very well aware that my lot is a happy one. In spite of Mary's death. I can speak to you of my feelings about being motherless because Mrs Bretton told me a little about your early life and losses. She was your godmother so I am your godsister-in-law! But now Lucy, I am pleased that yours is not a sad solitude, is it? I asked you if you minded solitude, but I can see for myself. Here we are – I am visiting you on a spring morning and see you have your work and other pleasures, soft breezes, sunlight in a green garden, music and books to lighten the heart. It has not been all tempest and shipwreck for you. Do not look so surprised that I recall your own images. They were strong and vivid.'

For a moment I could not speak, but I rallied. 'Perhaps I am a little surprised, but I think I understand your question. I had not thought of this before, but in telling myself my story – as we all do, I suppose, whatever we are saying – thinking myself so wise and thoughtful, facing life without illusion, perhaps I have not been altogether a faithful storyteller. Perhaps I have tended to see life too much in black and white, rain and sun, calm and tempest, shipwreck and safe harbour, comedy and tragedy.'

'The child and the mature woman?'

'Now it is you who smile at me. Yes, I must ask your pardon. These things – no, this way of reasoning – are the fruits, no, the faults of my roaming fancy. The troubles of my girlhood and perhaps my vocation – of which I think so much, which I cherish and value – have not helped me. I think of the world too much in terms of teacher and pupil, reason and passion, duty and pleasure. Stark opposites.'

'Do not suppose that I want to complain, or lament my lot, or criticise your judgement. It is something else. I am finding it difficult to put into words. Lucy, I do not want you to think I would have my lot in life changed, or that I envy yours.'

'Envy my lot? How could I think that?'

'I'm not sure if I can explain to you. I will try. You will understand that these are things I have not thought out in advance – or have only half-thought. I am saying some of these things for the first time. My life – my life with Graham and the children – is the life of a loving, a companionable, and a valuable wife and mother, and in it I feel fulfilled. Not only by its joys and rewards but by its pains, its shared pains, its anxieties, its endurance. But I see also that for many women, with less fortunate marriages, less wealth, less of a true and equal partnership, there may be frustration and loss, faculties rusted, dreams not realised. Even for me, from my safe harbour, there is the sense – and Lucy, this is knowledge, not fancy – that putting out to sea alone, without another firm hand at the helm, can bring its boons and benisons. Solitude and pain, to be sure, but work and independence. I remember long ago, when

we all met again here in Villette, I pitied you for having to work as
a teacher … to earn your bread. How young and ignorant I was
then! I do not envy you your life, Lucy, but I honour it, because
I can imagine its powers and its rewards. When you said just now
that you were a working woman, you looked confident, proud, even
exalted. You earn your living, every hour of your day and every day
of your life, and with all your resources, your busy hands and your
mind also. I see that a life like yours, not shaped in the ordinary
mould for women of our time, not crowned with the blessing – as
it is generally thought a crown and a blessing – of family, a good
husband and healthy offspring – such a life can be creative in the
way a man's life can be rich and creative. It can even be envied, in
a way, by women like me, who take the conventional path, whose
lives are sheltered and cast in the usual mould. But not sheltered
from pain and death, Lucy. Or age. I found a white hair when I
looked in the mirror yesterday. Dear me, I have made a speech. If
Graham were here he would smile. Perhaps that is why I needed to
be alone to say all this to you. I did not intend to say any of it, but
seeing the school, and even more, looking round this room – your
room – I am glad to have spoken. It has brought me a kind of relief
I did not know I needed. Thank you for listening so patiently. I am
so grateful. And so glad that we are able to take up our friendship
again, in spite of the years.'

'It is for me to thank you, Paulina, for undoing the simplifications
of my dangerous – my incorrigible, my quick-shaping, my over-
zealous imagination. And for giving me much to think about. New
thoughts. About your poor mother, and your feelings about her. I
am ashamed to think that in all these years when I have thought

of you and your father, I had entirely neglected to think of her. And you have started in me new thoughts about myself. About my advantages, about having my work and – perhaps not quite a home of my own, since this home is also a school, but at least a room of my own. You are right, of course, I do have that, and it is a rare and precious gift, not a poor second-best. I have not always thought of it so appreciatively. Thank you. When you were a very young child – such an original child, such an old-fashioned child – you had a way of putting your thoughts and feelings into vivid words, and asking me to tell you mine. That has not changed.'

'I have not quite done, Lucy. The thought also comes – forgive me if what I say now is an invasion of your privacy, but it is not a personal question I am asking, perhaps not really a question at all – but I have now and then wondered, especially when listening to the men at talk, if a man with a creative life, a life of social effort, of achievement in some art or craft or science, might not find in a different kind of union, a partnership in the workaday world, the world of Monday morning, benefits and aids that a good ordinary spouse and mother cannot offer, as she orders the house, and sees that the man comes back home from his labours to a pleasant house, well-behaved happy children, a warm hearth and a good dinner. This is something I have not really thought about, or thought about only in a confused fashion. I have shared Graham's ambitions and his thoughts and reading, and I have never been excluded from the conversation of his friends – as you know, when I lived with papa as quite a young girl he always encouraged me to read and talk to the learned company – but the truth is that the children and the management of a house and servants take all my time. When we have company I have to talk to the other wives – oh, you will not think me intolerant and critical, you will know what I mean. I read but it is often what Graham is reading and though I am glad to do that, I do not read for myself, or even think as much as I did when I was a girl, or even when I was first married. Well, I was still a girl then, a mere girl. I give everything I can to my husband and my children, but at times – for example, today, as I think about you and your work and your precious solitude – I know I am not using all my powers. And when you speak of a room of your own I suddenly realise that I am never – ever – alone. It is not that I am discontented or pine for solitude but now and then I seem to glimpse the possibilities of another kind of life. I do not know why I am saying all this. I seem to see my life through your eyes, as they might see mine, or perhaps because I can see – or imagine – your life. No, you need not look anxious. I will not go on. This is not an interrogation or a lamentation. I did not intend to make a speech! You do not need to remember any of it, only this, Lucy: it is a special pleasure to see you because I do not feel sorry for you.'

'Did you expect to feel sorry for me? To pity me, perhaps?'

'Do you know, I think I did. I can say that to you because you will understand. Words are so blunt. Please do not be offended. If I did expect to feel pity, I do not feel it now. On the contrary, I am glad for you and I am glad that I feel gladness. If I did not love my husband and children so much, I believe I should even envy you, Lucy. Dear me, I did not expect to say this.'

She was silent for a minute or two, and as I looked questioningly at her furrowed brow, the frown turned into a smile before she spoke again.

'I hope we can talk again. Like this. We will meet again before we go back to England. Perhaps I can persuade you to come and stay with us in Windsor, and get to know my children. But do not frown, I am not going to press you. I have no wish to urge a visit on you, and more important, I have no wish to probe and peer into the recesses of your life, present or past, my dear Lucy. Please to remember this.'

While she spoke my heart was full of an understanding I did not need to put into words. I was grateful for what she had said, and for what she had left unsaid.

We knew that conversation had come to an end, for the moment and the morning, so I stood up and smiled at the old friend who now seemed to be a new friend, 'Dear Paulina, shall we join the girls in the sunshine?'

Note

I have imagined some development on the part of Paulina Bretton, who marries when she is still very young, who shows signs of considerable intelligence and imagination, and the death of whose child Lucy Snowe mentions, though obliquely.

I am one of the readers who see the end of the novel as less open than it may appear, because of the prevalence of storm imagery throughout the novel, because Lucy Snowe the narrator is called Lucy Snowe, and because Charlotte Brontë herself wrote that she intended the end to be unambiguous, meaning what it says, in the mode of serious teasing present at the beginning in references to Lucy's early life and its losses, that readers who dislike tragic endings won't have   an unhappy ending – with the drowning of Paul Emmanuel – forced directly on them. I have left the superficial ambiguity untouched.

Edith Dombey and Son

'You addressed the daughter, I observed' said Mr Dombey … 'as Mrs Granger.'

'Edith Skewton, Sir, … married (at eighteen) Granger of Ours … a de-vilish handsome fellow, Sir, of forty-one.' From Chapter 21 of *Dealings with the Firm of Dombey and Son* by Charles Dickens

i

Father and Daughter

Two or three weeks had passed since Florence and Walter had called on Edith Dombey at Lord Feenix's house. Mr Dombey's health had greatly improved and he no longer spent long hours resting on his bed. One bright day in June, he was sitting with Florence in the drawing-room, looking at the springing green plants in the fernery, sunlight bringing out every fine frond, when he turned to his daughter and took her hand.

'Florence, there is something I want to say to you. You recollect, my dear, that when you returned from the visit you paid to Brook Street you brought back a spoken message for me and a letter. I think … I need not remind you … '

As Mr Dombey paused Florence looked at him and nodded encouragingly.

'It is hard to find the right words. It is hard to speak to you about this, Florence. But I find I have to speak, and I know you will forgive me if in any way I offend you. Perhaps I am anxious without cause: I must remember that you are no longer a child, but a married woman, with a child – a dear child – of your own. Well, then. When you came home from that visit to Brook Street you told me that your stepmother was not a guilty woman, as I had supposed, and on her behalf you offered a certain exchange of apology or penitence, as I saw it. I am sorry you look troubled, but I assure you that it will help me, if you can cast your mind back to the message you brought to me. It is a difficult subject for both of us.'

'Yes, father, but we must try to speak openly – to be honest with each other. Dear father, you know I found Mama in very great distress, without any clear intentions except to see me once again and tell me that she was guiltless of any sin against you. I told her you had lost everything ...'

'Ah Florence, that was not true, I had found everything, my child. I had found you.'

'Told her that you had lost all your money, and had been very ill and had nearly died, and she said I could tell you that if you could accept a share of the blame, she could do the same. Asked me if I was now very dear to you – and oh, dear papa, of course I said I was. I told her we were most dear to each other. She said that even though she knew you two would never meet again on this earth, now you had a living bond between you, and I was that bond.'

When he said nothing in reply, Florence looked at him with the old fear in her eyes, but looking keenly at her, he pressed her hand and said, 'Never fear, Florence, that I may return to my old jealous ways. On the contrary, recalling Mrs Dombey's affection for you has made me look back over the entire time of my acquaintance with her, and my courtship of her, in that black bitter time after dear Paul's death. The thought has made me look back to regret many things.'

He was silent for a moment, then resumed in a firmer voice, 'Now, Florence, I wish to answer Mrs Dombey's message. The letter, which you saw, and which I remember was addressed to you and to any other to whom you cared to show it, made it plain that no reply from me was expected. The letter, which you saw, repeated what she had asked you to tell me, but made no mention of the new living bond we shared, in you, and in truth she could only learn of that bond, of my deep affection for my dear daughter, from your own lips. I have come to think that both the message and the letter call for a reply. I am aware that none was requested; I felt assured that a measure of reconciliation, even of goodwill, would be inferred from my silence, but on reflection – long and painful reflection – I have decided to request an interview with Mrs Dombey. I wish to reply to what she said.'

'But papa, will it not cause unnecessary pain to you?'

'I think not, child. It may cause pain, but if so it will not be an unnecessary pain. On the contrary. Florence, I have spoken to you of my great sorrow for my neglect of you, my dearest child, but what you do not know – how could you? – is that I have to repent not only my coldness and harshness to you, my own child, but must also repent my treatment of my second wife. I know that you saw some of it, as I much regret, but not the whole, not the depths. I am doubly culpable, of being an unkind father and casting you off, but also of marrying a second time without love and with a cold calculation. And there is more, even more. No, my dear, do not look so distressed. It relieves my mind to be open with you. What I have to say is this. Looking back to my second marriage has made me look even further back, to my first marriage. I have to confess that it was not only to you and to your stepmother that I behaved wrongly. I was as cold and unloving to your mother, Florence. And Paul, your dear brother, to whom I was never cold, the child I loved so much … I loved him with a corrupted love … I cannot think of it without shame. I loved him deeply but I loved him as the son of the firm, as the "Son" in "Dombey and Son". But what concerns me here and now – at this present time – is my second marriage, my second wife. I wish to see Mrs Dombey and talk with her face to face. No – I think I know what you are going to say, that she told you we would never see each other again. I know we can never come together, to live together again, but there are things I must say to her. For the last time. Most solemnly and most truthfully. The letter she gave you, to keep or give to me, as you chose, was written in ignorance of the changes that have come about in me, and I want to speak to her, in fairness to her and to myself, because I have changed, as you know. The man she knew, the man she wrote about in the letter, the man she married, the man she left, was not the man I am now. I ask you to write asking if I may come and speak with her. I understand that she may not be willing to see me, but I must make the request.'

Seeing Florence frown anxiously, he went on, 'I am sorry to trouble you, my dear, but what you do not know, and what I am sure Mrs Dombey has never told you, is to her credit and to my discredit. Just before she fled my house, with the consequences we know, when we were bitterly angry and most hostile to each other, she begged me to listen to something she had to say, something of grave importance, and I agreed. Though not wishing to listen to anything that fell short of complete acquiescence in my wishes, still I agreed. But as I rejected so much else that was benign and reasonable in other people's behaviour to me, I refused and repressed the reconciliation – the friendship – she offered, refusing to recognise it, as I refused to accept my sadness about your poor mother, and my guilt about neglecting you. On that occasion your stepmother spoke of you with great affection, but – Florence, you know what I was once – what should have melted my cold heart only hardened the ice that bound it. I heard what she said but I put it away from me. We two, who should never have come together, can never come together again, but I want to respond, however belatedly, to the overture offered to me through you, and to complete that old conversation which I left uncompleted'.

'Papa, of course I will write to her. But her cousin, Lord Feenix, told Walter that they were going away, to the south of France. and I fear they may have left London.'

'Very well, I may be too late. In that case, I must accept that it is too late. But write at once, please. And there is one more thing, Florence. I want you to know that though your stepmother never loved me – and it is hard for a father, even a father who has been as unfatherly as I have been, to speak of a loveless marriage to a beloved child who is, thank God, loving and beloved in her own marriage – though she never loved me, she never lied about her feeling, never assumed a warmth she did not feel. She was always truthful, though I chose not to see the truth. I was the one who lied, who feigned a loving. In the unfinished conversation in her boudoir – I see that room now, as it was, strewn with her finery and jewels – she was always honest with me as I was never honest with her. That is why I want this meeting, to respect her and the truth, as she respected me and the truth. To explain that I know now that I drove her, if not to the deepest guilt, then to the fabrication of guilt. That feigned elopement, designed to shame me, led to a man's death. His most violent death. I am speaking the truth to you now, Florence, and I have not yet found myself able to pity him, the wretch I trusted, who did his utmost to ruin me in every way – to ruin my business, my honour, my marriage, my name.'

Mr Dombey rose and held his daughter close. Then they stood apart, and with tears standing bright in her eyes, Florence said, 'Before I write, papa, are you sure that you wish to see her – to see Mama in Brook-street? In that house? Would it not be less painful for you to have the interview somewhere else? Here perhaps?'

'No, my child. In no other place. Go now, please, and make haste to write. I will pray that I am in time.'

ii

Man and Wife

Mr Dombey and Walter drove the six or eight miles to the grey stately street in the west of London, and the carriage stopped at the tall house where Mr Dombey's unhappy marriage to Edith Granger had been celebrated. They were ushered into the house to be greeted by Lord Feenix, smiling and affable as he shook hands.

'My dear Dombey, I am delighted … I am relieved to see you well and mended, after your regrettable illness … and … all your other troubles. Good day, gentlemen, to you both. My friend Gay will have the goodness to wait and I will entertain him in my den until you are ready to return. My lovely and accomplished relation is waiting in the drawing-room, which is I fear in a somewhat bare and inhospitable state, as we leave England in two days.'

Mr Dombey bowed his head, saying, 'It is very good of you, Sir, to receive me at a time when you must be busied with preparations for travelling. I am grateful to you.'

He handed his hat to the manservant, and followed his wife's cousin up the dark staircase, dark though it was afternoon and midsummer. Lord Feenix stood back at the drawing-room door, smiling and murmuring, 'Yes, my lovely and accomplished relation is expecting you. I will be downstairs and she will ring for the servant to show you down when you have had your talk.'

The drawing-room was close and sombre, the sofa and chairs shrouded in white cloth. Edith Dombey was sitting by a table at the window, and rose to face her husband. She motioned him to a a chair at some little distance from hers, and resumed her seat. He bowed, and seated himself. She bent a little, apparently studying the pattern in the old red Turkey carpet.

He spoke slowly, a slight huskiness in his voice, 'Mrs Dombey, it is good of you to receive me. At this time. When you are so occupied with preparations …'

She surprised herself by looking up, and finding the conventional words without hesitation, 'I congratulate you, Mr Dombey, on recovering from your illness.' The tall and once upright figure was stooped, and as she made herself look steadily at him, she saw his hollow cheeks, the furrows and wrinkles on his brow and around his eyes and mouth. She wondered if she would have recognised him if they had passed in the street or in some crowded assembly.

She went on, speaking words she had sounded silently but never believed she would speak, 'I had thought we should not meet again, after I sent word by your daughter – by dear Florence.'

His eyes met hers as she pronounced the name and he in his turn found the right words, 'It was good of you to send that message to me'. He had thought of thanking her for forgiveness, but as he tried to find words he thought it had been neither forgiveness nor reconciliation that she had offered in her message or her letter.

Once again she found herself helping him, 'This is not easy for you – for either of us. Perhaps it will help if I repeat what I said to Florence, after she said certain words I cannot forget, words that are burnt into my memory: "I am very dear to him, and he is very dear to me". She said those exact words while still believing me guilty – oh, I was and am guilty, guilty of an act that must separate me from all my acquaintance, from this town and this country, an act designed in cunning and hatred, to punish at one stroke, the two men who had used me, or sought to use me. I was, and I am guilty, of having passionately resented you, for marrying me without love, knowing I had no love for you. I was, and I am guilty, of feeling ashamed of my wretched mother, who made my marriages, and made my mind, my disgraceful inclination. Do not think I cannot admit my own heavy fault, in marrying you; but before God, I am not guilty, as I brought myself to say to your daughter, of sinning against my marriage vows with that man. When I asked to see dear Florence, it was without any clear idea of what I would say to her. I wanted only to see her and embrace her for the last time, but when she told me that you were now very dear to each other, as I had always prayed you might be, when – we were all together – then I found I could tell her the truth about my detestation of him – of that man whose name I cannot bring myself to speak, but whom I used, as he used others, and as he wished to use me, to hurt and to shame you. And I could tell Florence, what she will have told you, that if in your present life, you could feel compassion for my past, and think less bitterly of me, I asked you to do so. I ask you now, I feel in my heart the pain and shame I hoped you would feel when I left your house, under cover of that feigned elopement – more bitterly than I felt it when I spoke to Florence. I am glad of it, and I can thank you for requesting this meeting'.

As she spoke, she pressed her hand to her bosom, and Dombey saw what he had never seen, tears standing in her eyes.

Dombey's voice was clearer and steadier as he replied, 'Thank you for your candour. In return, I must say that the purpose of this visit was not to request a repetition of your story, but to say what I would not have felt without Florence's forgiving tender love, what I cannot say to her, but only to you. In the letter which Florence showed me, you wrote that you and I would never meet again in this world. I understood the feeling that led you to write in that way. You asked her to say that when I felt proud and happy in her love for you, in her marriage, and in her children, I should repent the part you played in our false vows and matrimony. I have come to say that I feel the proud happiness in my child's love and forgiveness, and the repentance. I can only say it to you, the secret sharer of an unblessed marriage-bed. No, you need not speak. You understand that I could not say this to my child, or write it in a letter. Brought up as I was, with a man's sense of honour, and a man's pride – perhaps a false pride, I do not know – I have found it hard to admit all this even to myself'.

She nodded, her tears still shining but unshed.

'Mrs Dombey, please to bear with me a little longer. I have another reason for coming to see you. I have to ask your forgiveness for something else. You will remember the night I came to your room to impose my wish and will, and you asked me to listen while you appealed to me. I remember how calmly and slowly you spoke. I have turned over your words many times, in passionate contempt and in regret – ah yes, your words were powerful indeed; they were strong weapons. I can hear your voice, tuned to reason, to argument, to truth, begging me to confess the pains of the loveless and mercenary marriage which we undertook with open eyes, to seek with you some way of living without anger and distress, some way of showing each other some tolerance, even some friendship. You will remember – how could you forget? – what you said next, that you were asking this for the sake of three children. Three children. One of these was Florence, to name whom was to inflame my jealous hostility, and one was my dead son Paul, to name whom was to outrage my grief and possessive love ...'

'And the third', Edith said, looking at her husband, and speaking in a steady voice, 'the third child was my child, the child who was drowned when he was five years old, the child we have never mentioned. Is not that strange?'

'It is indeed strange – and most shameful. On the many occasions I have gone over that conversation – in which I played such a small mean-spirited part – it is those words that ring in my ear, as loudly as the hotel bell rang on that night in Dijon, when I arrived to confront you, as I thought, with your paramour – that cur and coward who fled to his death.'

'What else did I say about the boy? I know I spoke of the three children, but I do not remember my exact words.'

'You never spoke of your son by his name. You said only that we were connected by the dead, each "by a little child." Even though I was shutting my ears to your appeal, the words struck me strangely. You also said that we were connected by life, by Florence, but I could not accept that. I neither wanted her nor wanted you to love her. But that connection by death was something I began to feel and understand, though not for a long time. That was the only time you spoke of your son, before or during our courtship and marriage – our short bitter life together. Perhaps it was because you did not single him out, but linked him with my own dead child, but that was the one thing you said which I could not immediately reject, which bit into my conscience – which made me aware that I had a conscience, and had our marriage on my conscience. Even after I thought you guilty.'

'But why did those words of mine bite into your conscience?'

'Because I had asked Major Bagstock – the man who introduced us, your mother's *beau*, if you and Colonel Granger had any family, and he had told me that you had a boy who was accidently drowned, because of a neglectful nurse. That the death occurred some time after your first husband died. I hate to remember my question. I hate to remember his knowing nods and his knowing answer. Of course I needed to know. That you had given birth. To a boy. A healthy boy who died not of any illness but of drowning. You shudder, but you must have known that I would have asked, and that I knew.'

Mr and Mrs Dombey were silent for a full minute before he resumed in a stronger, louder voice.

'I believe the melting of my heart began with those words in which you reminded me of that dead boy – oh, I know what is in your mind. Yes, it took a long time to thaw that cold, but I have looked back on that moment many times. You had never mentioned your son to me, but I knew that you knew I had asked the question. There was no need for anyone to tell you. You were clear-sighted. You assumed that I would ask for information about your marriage and children, as a widower who had lost his son and wanted another, a male heir. But when you spoke of your son, in speaking of the two dead children who made a connection between us, it was brought home to me for the first time – though God knows how long it was before I would allow myself to think about it – that you had given birth to a child, a living child, that you had loved him, reared him, and alone, after your husband died in the second year of your marriage, as the Major informed me. Your son did not die as a baby, but lived for four or five years, a walking, talking, playing child – and then he had died. I never spoke of him. You never spoke of him. If we had spoken, everything might have been different. Before I saw you today, I prepared what I wanted to say – I wanted to recall the unfinished conversation in your boudoir, not to resume it and reply – it is too late for that – but to thank you for speaking on that occasion with such restraint and reason, for offering me friendship and reconciliation. But as I spoke to you just now, and warmed with the speaking, what I most wanted to confess was my hard heart, my refusal – though I had loved and mourned my own son so deeply – to think of your dead child as a human being who had once been alive. When we spoke in your boudoir, I was too occupied with my bitter resentment of you – and God forgive me – my black jealousy of your affection for my daughter – to ponder deeply what you said, but since we have parted your words have kept returning to me. More and more, of late. And is it not strange? Of the three children I have wronged, the one I never saw, and never spoke of until now, is the one whose little ghost comes back to haunt me. He comes more often now I have held my own dear grandson in my arms, and watched him grow, smile, and play. I cannot say any more. Thank you for hearing me out. I will leave you now, but I want to add that I wish you well.'

He rose from the chair and Edith went to him and held out her thin white hand, with its two heavy gold wedding rings. 'Goodbye, Paul. I wish you well. I am glad you told me. I am glad you spoke about my boy. I am glad you came '.

'Goodbye, Edith. I am glad I have spoken. I am glad we have spoken.'

He held her hand for a moment, and bowed over it. She walked across the room to the bell-pull with a stately grace, her black skirt sweeping the worn red carpet, her head held high.

Note

The scene in which Edith speaks to Dombey about her dead son, as she offers him the possibility of compromise and reconciliation, a marital modus vivendi, a scene more like Henry James than Dickens, and one which gives her character complexity and depth, is one whose insight and subtle drama I greatly admire. In this scene Edith also admits her guilt in marrying Dombey for money, and a similar admission by Dombey that he used marriage as a commercial transaction, is omitted from his conversion and the final liberation of his buried life. I wanted Dombey, and the novel, to revisit this scene.

Harriet Beadle's Message

She has given him a heart that can never be taken back; and however much he may try it, he will never wear out its affection. You know the truth of this, as you know everything, far far better than I; but I cannot help telling you what a nature she shows, and that you can never think too well of her.

I have not yet called her by her name in this letter, but we are such friends now that I do so when we are quietly together, and she speaks to me by my name – I mean, not my Christian name, but the name you gave me. From Chapter 11, Book 2, of *Little Dorrit* by Charles Dickens

As Amy came into her parlour she saw a dark handsome young woman, neatly dressed in black mantle and bonnet, who rose from a chair and said, making a little bow, 'Good morning, Mrs Clennam, I do hope you do not object to my calling on you'.

'Of course not, I am so sorry to keep you waiting. You are Miss Beadle?'

'Oh, it is for me to apologise, Mrs Clennam, for interrupting your busy morning, but I was anxious to see you alone. I asked your little maid to announce Miss Beadle, but I think you will have heard of me as Tattycoram. I knew your husband some years ago, first when we were in quarantine in the same company, in Marseilles, and then when he visited Mr and Mrs Meagles, and once or twice after I left the Meagles family. But you and I never really met, though we were once in the same room, you know, for a short time – the turnkey's room in the Marshalsea prison – where I had brought a box of documents from France. I wanted to keep in the background, and what was happening to the papers wasn't my business. I only knew they were important.'

'Oh, yes. I remember that we were all excited that day and I suppose nobody thought of introductions. I remember the occasion very well. I am so sorry, but I didn't recognise you at first. I was most grateful to you for bringing the box, whose contents were very important to me. I have often wanted to thank you. Now at last I can.'

Harriet's speech brought the past to Amy's mind – what she had seen with her own eyes, the papers she had burnt, evidence of the Clennam complicity in her father's financial ruin, which she had kept from her husband Arthur, and what she had heard of, her husband's first acquaintance with Mr and Mrs Meagles, and their beautiful daughter Minnie or Pet, now Mrs Gowan. Tattycoram had been Miss Meagles's maid and Arthur had told Amy how she had run away in rage and bitterness but had come back to be happily reconciled with the Meagles family.

She pushed the memories aside as her visitor said, 'I was very pleased to be able to do my friends, and yours, a service. I had been separated from them for a while, as you may have heard from Mr Clennam.'

'Yes … I have. ' Amy spoke hesitantly,' He told me about it, because he was very glad indeed when you decided to return to Mr and Mrs Meagles. Then we heard that you had gone to Italy to be with Mrs Gowan. I understand that you are still good friends with

her father and mother? They attended our little girl's christening
– it was very good of them after their own grand-daughter died
– but we have not seen them since and we have not heard anything
lately of Mrs Gowan.'

'Yes, they will not have talked about her, because they were
very anxious and very sad to be so far away when she has been in
trouble, and is not well. It is not very convenient for them to meet
in Rome – Mr Gowan is not fond of family visiting. Mrs Gowan
only writes very short letters now. I sometimes write for her. She
gets very tired. But I should like to talk to you about her now if you
can spare me a little time. I am very glad to meet you at last. For me,
you have been a girl in a story, but now I am beginning to feel that
you are a real person.'

'And I am glad to meet you. Do please sit down again'. Amy sat
down opposite her visitor, looking at her earnestly. Tattycoram had
been a girl in a story for her, but the story had been a painful one,
and she did not know how it was unfolding now.

'Mrs Clennam, though we never met properly I had heard about
you from Mr Meagles, who held you up to me as a good example,
a kind of model. You have heard of me as Tattycoram, but my real
name is Harriet Beadle. I don't mind the other now, as much as I
once did, but I like Harriet much better, and they all call me that,
even Mr Meagles, though now and then he forgets. But I can smile
at him and even make a joke of it when he does.'

'An example, oh, no indeed, I am no example', said Amy, 'except
in my family happiness – my husband and my two children and my
very great happiness. I should like to call you Harriet, if you would
please to call me Amy. Everyone does, except my husband, who

sometimes still likes to call me Little Dorrit, the name they called me when he first knew me, when I worked for his mother, and when I lived in the Marshalsea prison with my dear father, you know. I like him to call me that, for old time's sake. It reminds me of many many things that are very dear to me.'

'Yes, Mr Meagles told me something of your story – I hope you don't mind that he did – and he said how good you were. He told me that you had a hard life in your childhood, but that it had never soured your nature, as my beginning as a foundling most terribly soured me. You don't mind talking about all that, do you? I mean about the prison.'

'Indeed no. I never did mind. It was only my father and my broher and sister for whom the memory was painful. The prison was where I was born, and played, grew up, learnt to work, and lived with my family. When we left and travelled in Switzerland and Italy, I missed it very much. I was homesick for it. It had been my home – my first home.'

'That seems strange to me. I suppose because it is very unlike my feelings about the place where I was born – or rather where I was taken – and left – as a baby, soon after I was born. That was the Foundling Hospital, and it was a place I thought of as a prison. That was where I grew up and worked, and played – after a fashion. Thomas Coram built it as a home for poor children, whose parents had abandoned them. He was a kind good man, they say, but I hated it, and didn't like being reminded of it when they called me Tattycoram. Even now l don't like like thinking about it. For me it was never a home. I did not know what a home was. But you did not mind being born in a much worse place, a real prison, and growing up with the prisoners.'

'But you see the prisoners were my kind dear friends. My own father was a prisoner. My godfather was the turnkey. I used to play with his little boy. The prison was the place of my first and my dearest and my childhood memories. In the end my father died happy because he imagined he was back there in prison, not a rich grand man in Rome. I was luckier than you, Harriet – my mother died when I was very young but I had my dear father and my brother and sister with me.'

'You were not ashamed of the prison. And you liked the name Little Dorrit? You didn't mind not being called Amy? Or being called by your surname, as I was sometimes… called Coram, which I so hated, because it reminded me that I was a charity child. Mr Meagles told me that they disliked the 'Beadle' of my name, because of the hateful office of beadle, but you see, it was my real name, that I had been given, and I preferred it to the other.'

'I understand, but I got to like my nickname. Mrs Clennam and her servants in the old house didn't mean it unkindly, and when Mr Clennam, my husband, began to use it, when we first met and he was so good to me and my family, it was a word full of affection.'

'I have come to understand that Mr and Mrs Meagles meant Tatty and Tattycoram kindly, though in the end Mr Meagles admitted that it was a jingling kind of name. It made me feel I was being made fun of. And oh, I was jealous of Minnie Meagles, Pet, as they always called her. They meant to be kind in taking me away from the Foundling Hospital, my prison, and Mrs Meagles cried, they told me, when they came and heard us children singing. I was glad not to be a charity child, and I had good food and proper clothes, and they were gentle and most kind to me, always. But I was not taken to their home to be their child. I was their child's little maid. We were nearly the same age, and that made it worse, you know. Oh, I have come to see that I misunderstood many things, and the person you may have heard about – Miss Wade – encouraged me to run away, and encouraged my bitterness, I suppose to help her own bitter feelings. I did not understand that at first. But when I came to understand that she found it impossible to believe that anyone could really mean to be kind, I began to see that though I was like her in some ways, I was different too, and glad to be different. I was sorry for her, and I still am. She could never see kindness. She will never be happy in this world, and now I am happy. She could not change, and I did. But she understood what Mr and Mrs Meagles didn't understand – though they do now – what I felt, about being another girl's little maid, us being the same age, and about my name, and about keeping my temper. I did have a bad temper, and I still have. Poor Mr Meagles, he thought counting up to twenty would help me to control my temper, but every time he told me to count, in the kindest voice, it used to make me feel even angrier. I'm sure he meant well but though he was poor once, he had never been a servant, so he could not understand. I came to understand that he meant to be kind, and he has come to understand what I felt. I came to control my hot temper – oh, it was bad, and still is, deep down – because of course I could not scream or rush out of the room when I was with Mr and Mrs Gowan. And before I went to Rome, when Mr and Mrs Meagles's little grand-daughter died, and Mrs Gowan was so ill, and they felt so helpless, I began to feel sorry for them, as well as for myself.'

'And then you could help them, too, Harriet?'

'Yes, that was a great change from always being the one who had to be helped, and be grateful, so that helped me. And I was no longer their daughter's maid, doing things she could do herself. When they asked me to go and be with her, she really needed me, to help with the little boy, and to comfort her. I had to travel by myself, which I had only ever done once before, when I brought the box you wanted over from France. In Rome I had to manage not to show Mr Gowan that I had come from Mr and Mrs Meagles. And I had to help her, but as a friend, not a maid fetching and carrying, and being told what to do. We are friends, you know. Real friends. She calls me Harriet, and when we are alone I call her Minnie – she likes me to. We have talked about all my difficulties. Never about hers – she is too proud – but she knows I know what they are. She is no longer a petted child, poor lady. She misses her father and mother sorely but she knows they must be apart. She loves them very much, but she loves her husband and she feels her first duty is to him. I think it is easier for her to talk about my life than her own. And talking it over with her, and explaining, and looking back to the very beginning, we agreed that I had some cause for feeling sensitive – humiliated, even – about being a charity child, and then a maid, and being called Tattycoram. It was not all silly bitterness and hot temper.'

'Mr and Mrs Meagles called their daughter out of her name too. Some girls might not like to be called Pet.'

'That is true. Yes, I might have disliked that too, though I should have dearly liked to be petted. But never mind about me now, if you please. I have got over the trouble about my name, and my old quarrel with Mr and Mrs Meagles. They wanted me to go to Italy, for their daughter's sake. They thought she was lonely, and she is, because Mr Gowan has his painting, and many friends, and he needs to go into society. Mr and Mrs Meagles want me to come and see them, and bring them messages from her, and news of their grandson. It is because of her that I have come to see you. She has talked to me about you and her old friendship with you. It was at her request that I have called today.'

'I wrote to her after I married but she never replied, and I heard about the baby and her illness from her father and mother. But how is that you have you left her now, Harriet?'

'I have only left her for two or three weeks, to see her parents, with loving messages from her, and go back with loving messages from them. I shall not be coming back for some time. I shall not leave her if she needs me. She is not strong. But we have become fast friends, more than we ever were when I was her maid. I have helped her, with my company, and my talk of home. She has helped me too. I am studying Italian with her. She had teachers when she was a child, and on all our travels, and speaks several languages, but I didn't have any lessons after I left Coram's hospital. I am here now because she wanted me to come to see her parents and talk to them and take back news of home to her. Mr Gowan enjoys life in Italy too much to wish to come to England. So I am a link. But he does not really know about that. He heard that I had resented Mr and Mrs Meagles, and fallen out with them, and he was willing for me to come as his wife's companion. He does not know that her father and mother asked me to go. She was much alone, before I came. Even before her little girl died, she did not go into society with Mr

Gowan. It is convenient for him that she has my company.'

'Yes, I knew her and talked to her a great deal, first in Switzerland, at the St. Bernard Hospice where we met, then again in Italy. That was not long after she married. We became friends. She was on her wedding journey and I was travelling with my father and my brother and sister, after Father's money had been restored to him.'

Amy stared at the winter light and the street outside the window, as she remembered her first meeting with the beautiful young bride who had been Arthur Clennam's first love. He had never told her so, but she had read his looks and his tone and his words when he spoke of her, and she had written to him on her travels about their meeting in the Saint Bernard hospice when Minnie was alone in her room and ill, and their later meetings in Rome. Amy had known without being told that he loved Minnie because she loved Arthur herself, so she had read his secret because of her own secret. She had kept it, as she had kept her own secret. She wondered if sharp-eyed Harriet Beadle, when she was Tattycoram, had looked at Arthur looking at Pet, in the Marseilles quarantine and the cottage by the Thames, and if she had read his secret too.

'Mrs Gowan asked you to come and see me?'

'Yes, I have a message for you from her, and I have something to give you. The message is this — Mrs Gowan asked me to say that she is very sorry she never answered the kind letter you wrote when you were married, but her heart was too full, she said. She could not write. She asked me to tell you what she would have written if she had felt able to write. That you were married to a good man, and he was married to a good woman. That she could think of no two people who were so alike in their goodness, and who so deserved happiness. Those were her words. She repeated them, and I listened most carefully. This is the message. And here is the present for you that I have brought from her.'

'A present?'

Harriet Beadle, who had once been Tattycoram, picked up the large black reticule she had put on the table beside her, opened it, and took out a small brown leather box, which she held out to Amy Clennam, who had once been Little Dorrit.

Amy stood up, took the box, opened it, and saw a thin narrow circle of silver, too small for a woman's wrist. It was a child's bangle.

'Please to look inside the bangle.'

Amy put the box on the table, carefully lifted the bangle from its black velvet groove, and read the fine slanting words in silence, 'For my dear daughter.'

Harriet was watching her. 'Mrs Gowan had it engraved by an Italian jeweller for her little girl who died, soon after she was born. She wanted you and your husband to have it – for your little girl. With her love – her love for you, who had been so kind to her, and her love to your daughter.'

The question that sprang to Amy's lips did not pass them, but she looked doubtfully at her visitor, who shook her head slowly, as if to brush aside any scruple.

'She has been very ill, you know'. Harriet Beadle, who had been Tattycoram, looked grave, shook her head, and there was a long silence.

Then Harriet got up, took her bag and her gloves from the little round mahogany table, and said, 'Shall I say anything to Mrs

Gowan – for you?'

Still holding the silver bangle, Amy went over to her visitor, took her by the hand and said, 'Oh yes, I should be most grateful. I understand. I will not trouble her by writing. Please thank her. For the present and for the message. From both of us, of course. And I hope that some day you and I will meet again'.

When Harriet had gone, Amy walked up and down her little parlour, twisting the bangle round two of her fingers. She was thinking about many things. She looked beyond her room, and beyond the street, to think of the woman who had brought the bangle, the woman who had chosen the words engraved on it, and two little girls, one buried in the English cemetery in Rome, and one upstairs in the nursery. She thought of everything that had been said in the last half hour.

She looked further into the past, and saw another little girl, playing in a cobbled yard with the turnkey's little boy, then a prison attic where the girl, grown a little older, was getting her father's supper, then a cold midnight street where two poor girls huddled together in a doorway and made believe they were at a party.

She saw a bare room in a Swiss hostel where two young women were meeting for the first time, one raised on an arm as she lay in bed, the other holding a glass of water to her lips.

She saw the prison attic room where a young woman brought flowers for the man she loved and where he had told her he loved her. The man she loved so much, the good man she had married, the father of her children, who would be home in three or four hours and would listen as she told him the story of her morning, and told him about Harriet Beadle's message from Rome. He would pick up the small silver bangle and look at it. She knew him, loved him and trusted him, but she could not think what would be in his mind and what he would remember when he saw the inscription. What would he think? What would he feel? Arthur had once loved Pet Meagles, but now she paused, at the brink of his memories.

She asked herself another question. She felt free to ask it. If Pet Meagles, who was now Minnie Gowan, had loved Arthur Clennam instead of Henry Gowan, where would she, Amy Clennam, once Little Dorrit, be now?

Wherever she might be, it would not be in her small neat pleasant house in Fulham, with her children in their nursery upstairs. Those children would not exist. The house and the room would be there but with other inhabitants, without her and her loving husband, and her much loved children, and all the treasured possessions of her short married life. She looked round the parlour with its shiny horsehair sofa, its upright and easy chairs, its chiffonier with glass and china, its china stand with a green plant, its small bow-window with green velvet curtains, and its carriage clock ticking away the morning of her married life. As she looked hard the room and its objects became indistinct, and she looked through them into a past she had never known.

She breathed deep, and stopped at at the brink of her fancy. "I am being foolish', she said. But though she could not find the right words for her feelings, she knew she was not being foolish. She was seeing clearly and steadily. The past, in which Arthur Clennam loved Pet Meagles, before he met Amy Dorrit, was part of the history of her present happiness. No one was going to take anything away from her or her children. When Arthur looked at the little silver bangle, he would think of a dead child neither of them had ever seen, and he would feel for the woman who had chosen the words inscribed on it, whom he had loved, but neither his thoughts nor his feelings would turn away from her and their children.

All this was true, but they would never talk about it, and the silence would be something new for them. Love was not as simple as she used to think, when she found it, in a prison, in a great city, working for her father and sister and brother, or in a grand house, in another great city, caring for her father and sister and brother. Marriage was not as simple as she had thought. It changed every day. You could come to know other people a little better, but you could never know people entirely, even when you loved them and they loved you. You could come to know yourself a little better, and that knowledge, or that self, could change and surprise you.

She stood in a brown study, until footsteps and voices came to her from the stairway, and she smiled as a shrill cry, 'Mama, where are you? Come and play!' brought her back to the world of Monday morning.

Note

Dickens makes Tattycoram reject her 'generous' treatment by Mr and Mrs Meagles, under the influence of Miss Wade, but a modern reader will probably feel that the Meagles family was insensitive in their fostering – less than a fostering – of the Coram foundling. I have revised Tattycoram's simple return to the gratitude the Meagles expected, but allowed her to understand their insensitivity to her resentment as a charity child patronised and treated as a servant. I wanted to liberate her without disturbing Dickens's reconciliation or his critique of Miss Wade. And I have allowed Harriet Beadle to use her proper name.

Lucy Deane

… there was a tomb erected, very soon after the flood, for two bodies that were found in close embrace; and it was visited at different moments by two men who both felt that their keenest joy and keenest sorrow were for ever buried there.

One of them visited the tomb again with a sweet face besides him—but that was years after. From the Conclusion to *The Mill of the Floss* by George Eliot

i

Night Music

The young woman lifted her hands from the keys, and swivelled on her piano-stool to smile at the grey-haired man in his crimson armchair.

'Well, sir, was that to your liking?'

'I seem to remember the piece, my dear, though not the composer's name. Is it something you haven't played for a long time? By one o' your Germans? You know I never was musical, though I did play the flute when I was a young man. I always say trade opened my eyes to many things but you know I didn't have your expensive education.'

'No, papa, it was not one of my Germans but an Englishman,

who lived long ago, in the seventeenth century. Henry Purcell. It is something I haven't played for a long time. I am flattered that you stayed awake. I am glad you remembered. I'll make a music-listener of you yet.'

'Lucy, you learned puss, playing your old music seems to have brought back your old laugh and that is the sweetest music to my old ears. And you have put off the dismal look with those black dresses. I am so glad, my dear. And after all, you know it's been three years.'

'Yes, papa, I know. It was high time to shed mourning. The mourning garments, at least.'

She left the grand piano to kneel on a footstool by her father's chair.

'Ah child, I remember you sitting on that pretty little stool with the purple pansies – my dear mother embroidered it – and you leaning against my knee when you could scarcely walk. You used to make faces when I took my snuff. It seems like yesterday.'

'Yes, I detested the smell of snuff, and the dirty bits on your waistcoat. And I remember stroking the soft prickly velvet on the chair – I was never sure if I liked or disliked the sensation. But now Papa, please take a pinch of snuff or your second glass of wine, and then tell me why you are fretting instead of having your after-dinner nap. I know it's not really my piano and Purcell. I can always tell when there's something on your mind, you know.'

He turned to refill his glass from the decanter beside him, and put out a hand to touch her glossy light-brown ringlets.

'Yes, I know. You can, very well. But since you can read minds, I probably don't need to tell you my news.'

'It is about Stephen.'

'Yes. He is newly back from Italy and this afternoon he came into my room in the bank to speak to me. But his father had prepared me.'

'I see. And now you are preparing me.'

They were silent for a few moments, and she got up to sit down on the little stool. He leant to turn her averted face towards him and gently pinched her chin.

'Lucy, you don't need me to tell you. He wants to see you.'

'And you don't need to tell me why. Yes, papa, I will see him. I'm perfectly willing to see him. But I must tell you that it won't make any difference. All that is over. In the past. There are some things you cannot go back to. It would be impossible.'

'Lucy, my dear, you know all I want in this life is your happiness. But I am surprised that you are so unforgiving.'

She rose and walked across the long drawing-room to hold back a curtain and look out of the window, where darkness hid the lawn sloping down to the boathouse and the river. She could see only herself, in the lighted room. After some minutes she let the curtain fall, went back to the green piano-stool, and sat there looking at her father.

'Dearest papa, it has nothing to do with forgiveness. I am not unforgiving. I forgave him long ago. I forgave him even before the flood. It is true that when I forgave him I thought we might be together again one day. As we used to be. A poor silly dream. Now I know it is a dream that cannot come true, not because I can't forgive but because I can't forget. It is impossible that either of us should forget. If Maggie had not been drowned it would have been different – I believe she would have survived the scandal, recovered from her feeling for him, found something to do, some real work …'

'Work! What work could the wench ha' done? She would ha' married someone or other in the end.'

'Perhaps. I don't know. I think after Philip and Stephen Maggie would never have married. And women who don't marry can only teach, nurse or write, papa. Not teaching – she had done that and did not enjoy it. She was a great story-teller as a child. I loved her stories, about the toads and the ladybirds. She made a story out of everything. Who knows? Anyway I feel sure she would have outgrown – if that is the right word – grown beyond Stephen, grown away from her feeling for him. She had already left him, don't you see? – and after a while – yes – he might have turned back to me, just as he has done now, I would have accepted him and perhaps I would even have felt grateful. Perhaps we might have been happy. But since Maggie died in the flood, there can be no forgetting her, for either of us. No going back to where we were.'

'What do you mean by saying she'd have outgrown him? Stephen Guest is a man o' talent, a clever speaker, an educated man, a great reader.'

'Ah, it was Philip who put that idea into my mind. About Stephen being too shallow to comprehend Maggie. At the time – when he said that or something like it – I was offended, angry with him for criticising Stephen, whom I still loved so much, whom I had thought almost faultless, witty, very clever, far superior to me. I wouldn't listen. But Philip's words went on echoing in my mind. I have come to agree with him, and to feel that Stephen is not superior to me. I'm sure Maggie was much deeper and more imaginative than Stephen, and she might indeed have come to find that they were not well matched. Now I think, however, that I would have outgrown him – if that is the word – too. In fact, I already have. I do not want to sound vain, and it is difficult to say just what I mean, but I no longer look up to him. Oh, not because he loved Maggie and left me, but because I no longer think he is wonderful, or even exceptionally clever. I am very sorry for him; I can even feel a kind of affection for him. I wish him well. But I do not feel that I can share my life with him. I am sorry to disappoint you.'

'Yes, I am sorry, Lucy, and I am very disappointed.'

'Now, papa, one of the hardest things I shall ever have to do is to tell Stephen this, or some of it. Not my reasons – no, of course I cannot tell him what I have tried to tell you, but my decision. Please let him know that he can call; of course I will see him, though it will do no good. I cannot do as he wishes, but I'm not asking you to tell him that. I don't want to make you my messenger. I must tell him myself, I know. I won't like it, but if Maggie did it I can too.'

'Well, Lucy, I don't profess to understand all you say about your poor cousin and Stephen – that's going into deep waters, that is – but you've made your feelings about him quite clear. He will call at the bank early tomorrow morning and I'll send him on to you. His father will be sadly disappointed too. He had set his heart on you two marrying, Stephen settling down here and standing for parliament.'

'Ah, papa, we all set our hearts on things we cannot have, don't we? Mr Guest will not be disappointed for ever. I'm sure he will have a daughter-in-law one day but I do not think it likely that she will be Lucy Deane. Please don't be disappointed. Please don't look so downcast and sad. Think of Tom and Maggie. Think of poor Aunty Tulliver. Think of me. Remember, papa, it was very hard for me when I knew Stephen loved Maggie and I thought they had deliberately gone off together – eloped – but not as terrible as the flood, as the deaths, as the drownings, as the loss of my dear cousins. I loved them both, you know, very much, and it was the loss of my childhood. It broke my heart. Losing Stephen has not broken my heart. Feeling that difference made me understand myself better.'

Mr Deane got up slowly, and looked at her.

'Child, I must accept all you say about your feelings for Stephen Guest. There's no use arguing about feelings like that. But I can't help being sad about you. You were always such a happy child. I want you to be happy again.'

'Papa, once upon a time there was nothing in the world to make me unhappy. And you will think it strange, but now I am not only heart-whole, but I am happy – happier – now I've said all this and told you what I have decided. You see, I always knew he would come back and ask me. Poor Stephen, he is predictable in a way Maggie never was. Or Tom either.'

'Or you, Lucy. Now I have sometimes wondered. Did that poor lad have a liking for you?'

'Yes, papa, I'm afraid he did, though he never said anything. But I never had that kind of feeling for him so of course I never encouraged him, and you know Stephen began calling here and … paying court to me, as soon as I came back from France, and Tom stopped coming in the evenings. I was very sorry for Tom.

Sorry for him in a way I never was for Maggie. She had a very hard time, even as a little girl, and her death was an appalling waste, but you know there was much more in her life than in Tom's. He had that schooling in Latin and history, which was all so dull and meaningless to him, but she was a very clever girl, and she had her imagination … and books … and talk about Scott and Shakespeare with Philip. And I think her religion must have meant a lot to her though she never talked about it to me. No, papa, Tom never said anything about being fond of me, but I think he was. He was shy about some things. And very proud. When I lost Lolo he brought my darling Minny, and I remember how pleased he looked when I hugged the puppy and said he was just what I wanted.'

Lucy went up to her father and kissed him.

'I am a lucky man, to have a daughter like you. I used to be sorry I didn't have a son, but I know I am much luckier than Guest or Wakem, even though they may be better endowed with worldly goods. But don't frown, my dear, I don't like to see you frown. You are too young for care-lines. Lucy, I hope I'll live to see you a happy woman some day. In spite of everything that has happened.'

'Some day. Ah, father, who knows? I was frowning at the thought of Tom, and how little he had in his life. But he had the satisfaction of doing well in his work, and paying off his father's creditors, and even getting back the mill. Some day? I have learnt not to look far ahead. But I will say one thing to you. I have thoughts – oh, mere notions, vague and unformed – of being a wiser and more active woman than I have been or might have been if – if all that has happened had not happened. More like Maggie. Or more like what she might have been if she had lived. Don't look so gloomy, papa, or I'll hide your snuffbox as I used to when I was a child, and ask Dr Matthew to forbid port wine. As I told you, I want to help Ellen in the school for a little while, but I will be back with you quite soon, and I am not going into a nunnery, you know.'

ii

In a Painting-Room

'It's Lucy, Philip. May I come in? What a bright light from your glassed roof!'

'Yes, my father had it put in several years ago. What a pleasure to see you! Did you come alone?'

Lucy laughed, 'No, of course not. Papa happened to say at breakfast that he was calling to see your father, and I took the opportunity of his escort. Observing all the proprieties. Otherwise, I should have sent to ask you to come to me. I wanted to see you and your father said it would be all right to take you by surprise in this way. They need to have some talk about business so there is no hurry, if you can spare the time.'

'Of course I can. Welcome to my painting-room – I think you have never been here before. Thank you for climbing all the stairs. Please to rest while I go on with this for – just for a few minutes. That's the visitor's chair, with a cushion. Not that I have visitors, except for my father, and he did not come often until he was house-bound by this illness and hard up for company. And now he is sitting for his portrait. He would never agree to be painted before.'

As he spoke he painted, then stood back, looking at his work, and still holding the brush.

'May I look, please?'

'Yes. It is nearly finished. One more sitting should do it.'

She went to stand beside him in front of the easel.

The deep eyes in the heavy lined face looked straight at her with assurance and a kind of appraisal but on the full sensual lips was a smile that made her turn to the painter.

'I never realised before that you look alike – in some ways. It is not so much the features as that smile, amused, but a little wry, a little melancholy. Is he pleased with it, Philip?'

'He is, somewhat to my surprise. He says the smile is one he keeps for me, that no-one else sees. So the face in the portrait is one that only I can see. We've grown closer since his illness. Well, it goes back earlier, really … since I told him I loved Maggie, and he became reconciled to the idea. Not long before the flood. I can't talk about it; it cruelly roused my hopes. In spite of his dislike – his detestation – of Tulliver, I had actually brought him round to the idea of my loving her, perhaps even marrying her, by showing him her portrait. He talked to her once, at the bazaar, and thought her a fine woman. There it is, behind you, against the wall.'

'I didn't know you had ever painted her.'

'It was done several years before she died.'

As he was looking and speaking, he thought of his first portrait of Maggie, the miniature of her as a girl which he had shown her once, which was now by his bedside, in its case.

'She never sat to me for her portrait, of course. She didn't need to. It was done from memory. Let me bring it into the light, and put it on the easel. I can take father's portrait down if I'm very careful. There you are.'

'Ah, that dear old limp merino gown. And the golden light on her face and the folds of the dress. And that dark Scotch fir behind her. Philip, it is beautiful.'

'She was beautiful.'

'Yes, she was, but that's not what I mean. I mean your painting. It has something new about it. Both paintings have. I only saw some small water-colours you gave to a church bazaar. They were lovely, but these portraits are different. Strange. You have seen a gentleness, a softness, a humour – perhaps a self-reproach? – in your father. And you have caught the wildness in Maggie. What is she looking at? Did you know she once ran away to the gypsies when she was a little girl?'

'Yes, she told me the story one afternoon when we were walking in the Red Deeps, talking about Scott and Meg Merrilees. I remember how she laughed, as she talked about the funny little girl she was once. Yes, I suppose I know what you mean by her wildness, though I never called it that and I never thought of it quite like that. Of course I don't know what she is looking at. It is done from memory, and I remember the look. I had asked her to stand still for a moment, by the tree. She is – she was looking rapt. She was looking away. Looking past me.' Philip frowned, at Lucy's thought and at his memory.

She went on. 'I remember Maggie saying that she loved Purcell for his passion and wild fancy. I didn't understand what she meant then, and lately I have been playing some of his music, to remember her and try to feel what she may have felt. Stephen used to sing some of the airs and I accompanied him, but when I went back to the piano it was not Stephen, or myself, or even the old days when we all made music together, that I was thinking about, but Maggie and wild fancy. Now I seem to see a wildness in this painting – in her eyes, in her look. Do you understand? You painted it, after all!'

'I know she tried too hard to repress her imagination, her poetry. I didn't think of it as wildness.' He laughed but the laugh was not a happy one, 'Perhaps because I didn't want to. I could never accept her feeling for Stephen, and I could never accept that something was lacking in her affection for me. But I felt her capacity for pleasure – for poetry – for joy. If I am honest, for a passion I never awoke in her. I hated and feared the way she stifled her instincts, or tried to stifle them. Her austere religion was no good to her. And when those feelings – that wild passion – was roused, it was roused by him, by Stephen.'

'Philip, I hope you don't mind talking about her? When we met last I thought perhaps you seemed to avoid the subject, and now you are frowning.'

'Am I? No, not now. In fact, it is a relief, almost a pleasure. I am no longer so bitter about him, and you are the only one I can talk to her about her, Lucy. Father never knew her – only talked to her once for a minute or two. Not long before the flood. But I am an insensitive brute. Perhaps it is too painful for you to talk like this about your cousin.'

'No, it's not. Not at all. It is difficult to explain these things to Papa. And you are the only one I can talk to about her. Except for her Aunt Gritty – Mrs Moss, whom I visit sometimes. She loved Maggie dearly, and one of her children – Lizzy – reminds me of Maggie. Bright and dark, though smaller and slighter than Maggie. And not so absent-minded and dreamy. But I want to stop talking about Maggie for a moment, Philip. Today I am come to talk to you about myself, about my plans. You and I have not met for a long time – the old days of our glees and trios and duets seem like another life. As of course they were. Life seemed so pleasant and easy.'

She went back to the chair and sat down.

A flush came over Philip's pale face. 'You are come to tell me you are going to marry Stephen.'

'No indeed, Philip. You are quite wrong. I am not going to marry Stephen.' There was a long pause before she said, 'Last week I had to tell him so.'

'I am glad you are not going to marry him, Lucy.'

The clear light shone down on the man holding his brush, the woman sitting upright in the chair and the dead woman smiling on the easel.

'Glad? Ah, he was fond of you but I think you never really liked him, Philip. I remember when we talked once, after the flood. You said he wasn't worthy of Maggie.'

'He was not. I wrote to tell her so. She had been blind, mad with passion. I was not blind, though mad with jealousy. Liked him? I liked him well enough once, but you must remember that I loved Maggie. I think it was not only jealousy. I truly thought he was unworthy of her. I cannot like him.'

'Perhaps that's why you are relieved I am not going to marry him.'

Philip flushed again. 'You mean I don't want him to be happy. Perhaps. I haven't thought about that. No, I am no longer bitter, but I don't want him here, in this town, in my eye. But I am surprised at you, Lucy. You surely loved him very much? You broke down when they went off together in that fatal boat.'

'You're right. I did. But I recovered. Well, I recovered from that shock and sadness and jealousy. But dear Philip, you're only surprised because you think I am a suitable wife for Stephen – shallower, more decorative and much more conventional than Maggie. More ordinary. A sweet little thing. No, don't say anything. I know that's putting it crudely. I am not so sweet now, but you are right, about me as I was once. Three years ago, after the flood, when we were speaking about Maggie, whom we both loved so much, you were very bitter. You said that Stephen was superficial and conventional, fortunate in his good looks and physique, clever but unimaginative, and I was hurt. I still loved him, you know. I said to myself it was your pain and jealousy speaking. But the words cut deep into me, and when I looked back over our acquaintance and courtship, I began to see – oh, not only that Stephen was all the things you said, but that I was too, Philip. What I thought of as love was shallowness attracted by shallowness. Life was like a dream. Singing and boating and dancing and dressing up and playing at love. I was young and stupid, and so was he, in spite of all his travel and education. And I looked back over my times with Maggie, too. They used to call me the belle of St Oggs and I rather enjoyed all that but I think – I believe – I am more like Maggie than you thought. I hope I am. I recall talking to her just before the flood. I went to see her – in secret, without telling Father – to tell her that I didn't believe the stupid wicked gossip, and I knew she never wanted to betray and hurt me, and to assure her that I was not going to die of a broken heart. I knew she was strong and I was weak, because I couldn't stop loving Stephen, and she had the strength to send him away. I told her that. But I was wrong. I did stop loving him, you know. I really did. You'll think it singular – no, perhaps you won't. Philip, you can understand – but you know I thought the less of him for coming back last week and asking me to marry him.'

'Because you thought he was insincere?'

'Because I thought he was sincere.'

Philip smiled one of his rare smiles. 'Ah, I see. Yes, I see you have changed, Lucy. But if he was sincere, he must have been hurt.'

'Yes, poor Stephen. But don't you see, just as he recovered from loving Maggie – at least recovered enough to want to marry me – after a while he may recover from this setback too, and find someone else?'

'You're right. He will tell his bride the tragic story of his first love and bring her back to put sweet spring-flowers on Maggie and Tom's grave.'

'Don't laugh like that. Don't be harsh, Philip. Oh no, it could never be like that. I am critical but I am not cynical, and I believe there was something truly tragic for Stephen, which he will not forget. In loving Maggie and losing her – and so terribly. The day after our last meeting, when I refused him, he wrote me a letter saying that he understood my decision, and honoured me for it. I was surprised by what he wrote, or perhaps by the way he wrote it. He had begun to see that I had changed, he said, and he respected the change, but he was not taking my answer as final. Not because he was vain or stupid but because he believed that we cannot predict our futures. He said he had changed too, more than I realised. Perhaps that is true. I don't know. I did not reply to the letter. He wrote that he did not expect an answer.'

She got up. 'Perhaps I should not have told you all this about Stephen. I did not mean to. I am come to say goodbye. Next week I am leaving St Oggs. I am going away for a little while, to Brussels, where an old friend of mine lives – she was at school with me and Maggie, before Maggie had to leave and Uncle Tulliver lost the lawsuit. Ellen's father died and left her a little money and she has started a school there: I am going to teach the little ones English and music, and try to be a useful woman. I haven't any proper experience but I like the Sunday school, and I've always liked looking after small animals! I may not be any good at teaching, but I am being cautious and only planning a short stay. Papa isn't getting any younger, but Miss Mills – you know she came to keep house after Aunt Tulliver left to live with the Pullets – will take good care of him. I'll come home for Christmas. I may take Lizzy Moss back with me if there seems to be an opening in the school for her to help and learn. There's nothing but drudgery for her at home.'

'I feel even more surprised, Lucy, but I think I'll be glad for you as well as for myself when I have thought more about it. Thank you for telling me all this. Perhaps you will be a good friend and write to me.'

'Of course I will. And in the summer I'll come to see the portrait of your father in the Academy.'

'Who knows, perhaps you will. I am looking forward too, you see. At least I find myself a little less inclined to burn my canvases. Goodbye. You know, some day I should like to paint you, Lucy.'

'Ah, you never suggested that before. I wonder: "A Portrait of Lucy Deane." When I may have grown a little wiser. With timelines on my face. Thought-lines too, perhaps. Perhaps my face will become more interesting.'

'It is interesting now.'

She laughed, 'I admit I am more interesting to myself than I was once. I used to busy myself all the time with plans and hopes for other people – Maggie, you, Stephen – without really knowing anything about them. I certainly did Maggie and Stephen no good. Or myself. I suppose fancying futures for other people was easier than thinking about my own life, which I simply accepted. I took it for granted. Perhaps I don't know myself very much better now. But a little better. I've thought about everything – myself and other people, even my father – in a way I never used to. But I don't feel familiar enough with myself, when I look back, or when I think about the present, to be confident about the future. I think all I know is that anything – anything – can happen, except what you think will happen. Do you know what I mean? I'm not sure I do myself!'

'Yes, I think I do.'

Lucy looked up at the large sky-light: 'We see the river while you see sky. And its light on your pictures. You have something to feel confident about, Philip. In the present and in the future too.'

They shook hands and she smiled as he held the door open. 'Goodbye, and thank you for listening. No, please don't come down all these stairs. Go back to the easel, while your light lasts. I can manage on my own.'

Note

I have called Philip's studio a painting-room, because that is what George Eliot called it, perhaps not using the word studio, used for the workplace of professional painters in *Middlemarch,* to reflect Philip's seclusion and modesty.

Dorothea's Daughter

... there came gradually a small row of cousins at Freshitt who enjoyed playing with the two cousins visiting Tipton ...

Mr Brooke lived to a good old age, and his estate was inherited by Dorothea's son, who might have represented Middlemarch, but declined, thinking that his opinions had less chance of being stifled if he remained out of doors. From the Finale of *Middlemarch* by George Eliot

It was a fine May evening and Dorothea Ladislaw was reading in the small front parlour which looked out on to the river. Every now and then she put down her book to listen, until at last there came the sound of a cab drawing up at the front door. She got up eagerly, put her book on the lamp-lit table beside her, and went to the parlour door. Not hearing the knock she was expecting, she resumed her seat but not her book, a surprised frown on her high forehead. It was more than a quarter of an hour before the knock came, loud and repeated, followed by steps hurrying along the passage, two raised voices, laughter, and then the parlour door was flung open and her daughter was in her embrace.

'Mother, I am so happy to see you, and to be home. Home, home at last, sweet home!'

Dorothea stood back, smiling, then holding her daughter at arms-length to look at her. 'And pray what have you been doing since the cab drew up?'

'You have such quick ears, Mama! Well, I asked the driver to wait for a minute or two while I got out to look at the river. I have missed it so much and I wanted to see the reflections in the water. I didn't think you'd be listening. But you don't mind, my dear and most tolerant mother, do you? It was only five minutes.'

'Well, I did wonder after I heard the cab draw up and you did not appear. Yes, of course I was listening. No, of course I don't mind. So you missed the black Thames and foggy Chelsea and these narrow rooms? When you had all the wide pastures and the grand parks and avenues of Freshitt and Tipton!'

'Please to remember that I am a London girl, not a country mouse!'

'I am not likely to forget, when you don't tell us the time of your train and insist on such independence as coming all the way from Euston to Chelsea in a cab on your own!'

'I knew Papa would be busy working on the paper and I didn't want to bring you out to the noisy station. And it is a summer evening! And it is 1860, you know! And I love what you call my independence!'

'Dear child, I like you to love it. As you know. Ah, it is so good to see you. Yes, Papa will be late, but he promises to come as soon as he can. This is the second number, and he is anxious that it should do as well as the first. We were very glad you liked it. Now take your things off – throw them on the sofa. Are you hungry? We'll have something on a tray.'

'How delicious, one of our dear old comfortable cozes. I promised Phoebe to come down after supper – whenever that was

— and have a good talk before she goes to bed, with messages from her sister at Tipton and all their folk, you know.'

'And I hope you bring messages from all our folk, too?'

'Of course I have. Pocketfuls of love from Hal and Emma and Aunt Celia and all the cousins and the prodigious babe, who is almost talking and the apple of his father's eye, not to mention that of his Aunt Margaret in all her dignity of new aunthood. Now sit down, Mama, and take off those spectacles, because they pinch your nose and make you look severe, and let me take my hat off and sit on the floor as I used to. That's better. I hate hats. Now, let me babble away.'

Dorothea bent and turned her daughter's face towards hers, smoothing back the rippling golden hair. 'Yes, you are babbling, and you are also blushing. Has something happened?'

'Nothing at all. Well, not exactly nothing. Now you look severe even without your spectacles.'

'No, serious perhaps, but surely not severe. Margaret, is it John?'

'Oh Mama, you are a witch! You may be shortsighted but you are clairvoyante — there's no keeping anything from you. It is good that I like telling you things. Some of my friends say they cannot talk to their parents. I am lucky that I can. Yes, I'm afraid it is John. Was, rather. But you do not look surprised?'

'No, I am not surprised, nor will Papa be.'

'Why not?'

'Never mind that for the time being. Please to tell me what you want to tell.'

'Well, Johnny has been on the brink so many times, and I've

wanted to keep him there. On the far side, hoping he would not cross over. I got rather good at it. But I suppose taking his degree and leaving Cambridge brought it on. So he jumped off the brink and took the plunge. And I had to say no. It was hard, Mama, he seemed to take it for granted that I shared his feelings, that it was the same as when we were children, and he sent me a valentine, you know, a funny little poem about carnations or roses. I remember his drawing of flowers that could have been either. But once it sank in, he was very good. I could see he was trying not to make it hard for me. I know he is hurt and disappointed, but I think his heart is only a little broken, and I am sure that by and by it will mend. But tell me, how did you know that I should refuse him?'

'I did not know, but I wasn't surprised, because you are so different from each other. And this is not the first offer you have declined, is it, my dear? But I certainly did not predict anything. Indeed I was a little afraid that the past would tug at you, but I trusted your intelligence and your independence. John wants – and I think perhaps he needs – another kind of wife, one he can lead and influence. I won't venture to say anything about your wants and needs but I think they are very different from his.'

'But you know, Mama, it wasn't only John. Everything seemed to come all at once, you know. Staying with Hal, seeing Emma and my nephew, going over to teach the little girls drawing and baby French, oh it was all fun and fascinating for a time but by the end I knew I didn't want to spend my life in nurseries and schoolrooms. Or great houses. I was so glad when Miss Brown's mother recovered and she came back. That brought on the proposal, because I decided to come home almost at once. And oh Mama, though the fields and

parks are wide – I loved the early morning ride through the lanes
to Freshitt, and the hedges with the cow parsley and elderflower – I
knew that for me the life would be too narrow. Aunt Celia says she
pities us living in a street, but I would not want her life. You see why
I had to go and look at the river straight away. It's one of my first
memories, looking at the river, along with the memory of you and
Papa showing us the Great Bear from the garden window.'

'Did your uncle and aunt say anything about your refusal? I
suppose they knew.'

'Yes, of course, you know Johnny. Heart and heartbreak on his
sleeve, in full view. Everyone could see what had happened. I think
my aunt put it down to his being so much younger, though she
was disappointed and rather tearful, and Uncle James said he was
sorry, but he was very kind. He said a strange thing as I was saying
goodbye. He kissed me, and I was surprised – usually he doesn't
make a show, you know, and he gave me a long look and said I
might take after Papa but I had more of you in me than met the
eye. I wasn't sure what he meant.'

She looked at her mother, who paused before she replied. 'When
we were both much younger your uncle and I did not always agree
about things. As we grew older and wiser we agreed to differ.'

Though the mother and daughter had always talked freely to
each other, what Dorothea had said was the truth, but not the
whole truth, about her relation with her brother-in-law, nor was it
all she thought about that little speech he had made to Margaret.
She wondered if he made the speech because it was likely to be
repeated to her.

'Do you know, Mama, I've sometimes thought Uncle doesn't

really like Papa? Is it about politics?'

'Politics and everything else, Margaret. They differ in every
way. In mind, feeling, background, education, religion, politics, of
course – everything.'

'Was Uncle James a friend of Mr Casaubon?'

'Oh dear no! They were very different men also.'

She had never before heard the name of her first husband on
her daughter's lips. She drew her shawl more closely around her
shoulders.

'Mother, are you cold?'

'No, a goose was walking over my grave, as Phoebe would say.
Margaret, has someone been talking to you about Mr Casaubon?'

'No, not really, but one day Aunt Celia and I called at Lowick
and there were workmen – painters I think – in the drawing-room,
so we were shown into the library, and there was a portrait of Mr
Casaubon hanging by the window. The sun was lighting it, and I
recognised the signature. I remarked that it was a strange, striking
picture and painted by Papa's friend, Mr Naumann, whose name I
knew from your portrait in the study. My aunt told me it was Mr
Casaubon, in the costume of Thomas Aquinas.'

'Yes, of course, the artist was Herr Naumann. He painted that
likeness of me when we met in Rome. At the same time as the
Aquinas portrait. I was supposed to be Santa Clara.'

Dorothea closed her eyes, and quick, quick, she was back in the
Roman winter, on her wedding journey. She was seated in the big
light modern studio, with the warm stove, the two canvases and the
three men, her first husband resting in an old carved chair, looking
across at his half-finished portrait on an easel, a wintry smile on his

thin lips, her second husband walking round restlessly looking at the pictures on the walls and humming a snatch of some song, the painter holding his brush and looking intently from her to another canvas, back and forth. The December sunlight shone on his dove-coloured blouse and maroon cap, and on the two portraits, their paint fresh and wet.

She opened her eyes on her little parlour and her daughter's bright questioning face.

'Adolf Naumann, yes. Some time after your father and I were married Herr Naumann brought it to London, and gave it to us as a present. I never greatly cared for it. So was that all your aunt said?'

'Yes, that was all. I thought Aunt Celia looked as if she was going to say something but she didn't. No, the picture makes you look too saintly, I always thought. And you never cup your cheek in your hand, like that. You are not like a saint, Mama. I don't like saints.'

'Margaret, I once told you that my first marriage was not happy, and that is one of several reasons why I am glad you are not going to marry your cousin.'

Margaret was thinking that John Chettam did not look at all like Mr Casaubon, as her mother continued, 'There are many kinds of unsuitable marriage. But I hope you are not feeling too unhappy about John.'

'Unhappy for him, yes, but not about him. No, for myself I am glad, I hope not too selfishly. Though I too am not at all saintly, dear Saint Clara. As you know. Mama, I've never asked you before but it's just popped into my head. Why did you choose a saint's name, Theresa, for my first name?'

'Theresa Margaret Ladislaw. That was your father's idea, a kind of affectionate word-play, because it is a little like my name. Not because you are like Saint Theresa in any way. I hope you are not.'

'I'd never have thought of that. Just like Papa. Mama, I know I am not clever about politics and – oh, good works – like Papa, or you, but there are so many things I want to do, and at the moment they all seem to be crowding together in my head. I suppose it is because I have come to know some of the things I do not want to do. Certainly not to be a nun or a saint. Neither of us – you nor I – has a saint's temperament.'

'Saint Theresa was a most unusual saint, you know. She was a holy woman but she was also a clever and competent one, and she founded a great order. But what do you mean about knowing what you do not want to do?'

'That is easy. I do not want to get married, to Johnny or to anyone else I have ever met. I do not want to live in the country. I do not want to be rich and have a big house. I do not want to be a governess to my cousins or to anyone else. I do not want to paint landscapes and sketches of babies. Oh, I don't mean that I am ambitious or full of plans and great ideals, as Aunt Celia says you were when you were young. I do want to work, to do something. Staying down there near Middlemarch with the family – Aunt Celia and Uncle James and seeing the grand-children, and now Hal and Emma and the baby – where life is so different from our life, being away from London, missing the talk about politics and Darwin and schools and what might be done to improve the world – all that has stirred me up, and I feel excited, disturbed, eager, wanting to be different, to be busy, to read more, to know more. Oh, it all sounds very vague. Mama, what can I do? I was pleased to have Uncle's legacy, but I want to do something with it, and I have no idea what. You and Papa have quite enough, and you both work and do good. But what can I do? I want to go on with my French and German and my painting, but I'm not good enough to be a translator or a real painter. I'd like to do something noble, and work for other people like Miss Nightingale but I can't bear invalids and all that, and the very thought of blood and bandages makes me feel faint. Nothing is very clear to me. It has been seeing what I do not want that has started me wondering what I do want. Do you understand? I'm not at all sure I do myself.'

'I think I do, but remember that there is no hurry. You are young.'

As she spoke, Dorothea wondered if it was true that there was no hurry. It was nearly thirty years since she had felt like her daughter, longing to do something, asking herself, 'What can I do?', and never finding the answer, longing to right some of her world's wrongs, but not seeing how, having a little knowledge but not enough, having a little money and not knowing what to do with it. Those old riddles were with her still.

'When I was your age I felt like that – I was always wondering what I could do – but I was much more conventional than you are, Margaret. And also too unrealistic. Knowing what you do not want is a good start. I knew what I wanted, but not what I did not want. And I was too precipitate, seizing at the nearest thing – in my blundering blind way. I am glad you know that you must look and think and not rush into decisions.'

She did not say that the nearest thing she had seized had been marriage to a man she had hoped to help in a great work.

Margaret smiled. 'I promise not to be rash. I do not have impulses to seize things. I wish I had. I don't know enough and I haven't done enough. You had ideas and ideals but I have not. I do not have any large view of the world. I thought I would like teaching, perhaps because you and Papa taught me so well, but I did not like teaching small children, you know. Sometimes lately I've thought I should like to write, but I haven't anything to write about.'

'Papa and I have enjoyed your long letters, full of stories about the family, and full of fun. It was like hearing you talk.'

'I loved writing to you both. Perhaps that's what put the thought of writing into my head. That and Papa writing about his hopes for the *New Monthly,* and seeing the first splendid number. I don't know. I haven't read enough, only novels and poetry. I know you used to read books about labourers' cottages and architecture and all that, and I like hearing you and Papa talk about politics and the Ragged Schools, but I haven't got that kind of mind. I feel life is full of openings and possibilities, but when I try to think what I could do, teach or write or nurse, nothing seems within my reach. And time does rush by. Oh dear, what a moan! But I do feel that it is good to be home. I loved driving through the streets tonight. London is so much fuller and wider than they think down there in their great houses, isn't it? Yes, Hal is becoming a country squire, though it suits him, and he has always liked country things, and used to love riding over the estate with Uncle Brooke when he was a little boy. The tenants like him. I wouldn't change him, or dear Emma either, though she is a besotted mother. She still reads novels, but her talk tends to wander back from the characters in books to the baby's future – I am glad to see him so happy and rosy, not like the London children, and I love them all, but I would not change places with them.'

'Dear Hal. I was sorry he has given up that idea of standing for election, but he has always liked the open air, and horses. And he is being good about the cottages. I think Papa giving up his seat, and then giving up the law for the paper, made him feel free to make his own choice. I think he will be a good landlord. He is improving life for the tenants, as you have seen. Uncle Brooke kept to his own ways even though he was such a great age. Your father was impressed by that wicked letter – a little unfair, though – you sent us with the caricature of Hal the fat squire asleep over his port.'

'That was only a tease. I knew Papa would laugh but I was a little afraid you'd be shocked at the degeneration of your sweet little water-colourist.'

'Come now, child, when did I ever care much for pretty sketches?'

'True, you have always cared more for good causes than art, you Philistine. Not that my caricatures are any better than my water-colours. I love drawing and painting but only as amusements, as I practise them. I shall always care for art, but I mean to care for other things too, if I can. Papa does, after all. Oh, it is so much easier for a man, Mama, you know that. When he was young Papa could travel, and then try everything, painting and poetry and politics and law, and end up now as an editor and a writer.'

'Yes, but remember that Papa has not had everything he wanted. He had great hopes of making a difference when he first went into parliament, but in the end real reform still seemed to him and still seems – as it does to me also – out of reach, something we are unlikely to see in our time. He gave up his seat in parliament, and went back to the law, which he never liked but which at least brought in a little income. He did not like to rely too much on my money. But that disappointment about politics did not mean giving up all hope and caring about the world. He will never do that. Nor will I. Now he and his friends have come to hope that we can work for small reforms, improvements in education for the poor, and working conditions for children, through this paper. As Mr Dickens does. It is strange to think how things come about. It was Uncle and his Middlemarch paper the *Pioneer* that started Papa's interest in political writing, and then Uncle's legacy to me made it possible for Papa to give up law and start again. But of course you are right. It is much easier for a man. In spite of Miss Nightingale, there are not many opportunities for women. I found that in my own life. Things have not changed very much in thirty years. When I was your age – no, younger – I had a secret longing to be a man, to improve life for the poor labourers, even to write books.'

'Oh, Mama, I understand. But do you not think things are changing a little, however slowly? Before you were married you never travelled by trains and cabs, by yourself, did you?'

'Indeed I did not. When I was your age the railway was only just coming to Middlemarch, and a young woman of my class only travelled in a carriage. But that is only a small change in a woman's life, is it not? Though perhaps we do not see how important small changes are. I suppose they come about without us noticing them, or seeing their importance.'

Margaret did not reply but scrambled to her feet, stretched her arms, and walked up and down the long narrow room several times, until she stopped to pick up an open book lying on her mother's lamp-lit table.

'Oh, Mama, you are reading this? Emma had it from Mudie's as soon as it came out. How did you get hold of it? I am surprised – you always say you don't care for novels. You don't like Dickens and Balzac as Papa does. You don't like Scott. Hal and I used to love it when Papa read to us but you never listened. He used to do the characters in different voices.'

'Papa gave it to me. He has written a long review for this next number. He said even though I do not care for novels I should read it. He was sure I would like it. He said every woman should read it, so of course I could not regard myself as an exception.'

'Mama, please to be serious.'

'You and papa always say I am too serious. I was amused at his insistence, but I am serious about the book.'

'I should think so. Emma said it was too painful but I thought the painfulness was a way of telling the truth. I found it wonderful. Of course it is terribly sad – no, not sad, that is too weak a word – I should call it tragic.'

'Don't say any more. Papa said he would not say anything until I had finished. So far I can't sum up what I feel in words. I am some way from the end, and at the moment I feel as if it isn't a novel at all, but as if I am in it, watching a piece of life, a real life, no, real lives. Seeing her – no, seeing two young people growing up like you and Hal, seeing them struggling and threatened, not knowing what they are threatened by, wanting to help but unable to reach out to them. I'm afraid of what is to come. I felt that from the beginning. Especially for her. It is not like any other book I ever read. It is not like fiction but like life tearing through the pages. Tearing the pages. Tearing the heart.'

'Yes, it is fiction but it is like life. No, it is life. A woman's short life. She did not know what to do with her life, did she? Any more than I do. Someone told Emma the author was a woman, and I began to read it again, thinking about that. She must be a woman who has lived much longer than I have, and has known sorrow. Oh mother, nothing has happened to me. Perhaps it never will. That story must have come out of real experience – a woman's tragic experience.'

'Whatever you do, pray don't tell me anything about the end.'

'Dear me, mama, now you are talking like a novel reader!'

'This is not like a novel. Margaret, though we cannot expect life to be without some sadness, because I am your mother I hate to think of you suffering or grieving. Like every life, mine has had its sadnesses, though I have seen far greater sadness in some lives that have touched mine, and I am blessed in my marriage and my children. I regret things I did when I was young and foolish, but nothing in my life has been tragic. What a black word! And what a painful talk we are been having. That's enough now. Dear me, perhaps all this comes of reading novels, even serious ones that try to tell the truth about real tragic life. Let us think of some other subject. Listen, I think I hear Phoebe coming with the supper tray.'

Note

Dorothea's daughter is an unknown quantity, a speaking silence. George Eliot chose to give Dorothea and Will two children, telling us that their son inherited Tipton Manor from Dorothea's uncle, but being as silent as she can be about the second child while making it clear that she is a daughter. Perhaps she chose to create her, but in this minimalist way, because she wanted to put a woman into Dorothea's – and the novel's – future but to imagine neither too little nor too much for her destiny. I think of her as being born sometime in the mid-1830s (at least fifteen years later than Mary Ann Evans, who was born in 1819) and in her twenties at the time of my story, which is set in the early sixties.

'Liza-Lu Durbeyfield

People marry sisters-in-law continually about Marlott; and 'Liza-Lu is so gentle and sweet, and she is growing so beautiful. O I could share you with her willingly when we are spirits! If you would train her and teach her, Angel, and bring her up for your own self! … She has all the best of me without the bad of me; and if she were to become yours it would almost seem as if death had not divided us…. From Chapter 59 of *Tess of the d'Urbervilles* by Thomas Hardy

'Poor 'Liza-Lu, you look exhausted. The sun is setting, and we have walked ten miles at least. I'm not sure what this place is, but look – there is a cottage over there by the sheepfold, and if you rest here on the stile, I will go and ask the people if they can give us a night's shelter.'

Liza-Lu was glad to rest, putting down her bundle, leaning against the stile and watching Angel walk towards the small house. She closed her eyes in sorrow and weariness, and opened them to see Angel running back. He took the bundle and they walked to the house together.

'I spoke to a nice old woman and her husband, a shepherd, and they will take us in. I've explained that you are my sister-in-law, and that we are looking for work after trouble at home. She says you can share her bed, because her man will be out with the sheep all night, and I shall sleep in the hayloft.'

The old couple greeted them warmly, and all four sat down to bread and cold meat, cheese and beer.

'Have you come far, my dears?' asked the shepherd's wife.

'From Wintoncester', said Angel.

She looked at 'Liza-Lu's reddened eyes and black frock, shook her head and gave a little sad smile. ''Tis a good step. You must be clemmed. Make a proper meal now.'

'Yes, the young 'oman looks fair to drop,' said the shepherd.

In the morning, after a night's good sleep, they breakfasted on bread and bacon, and took their grateful leave. The old woman stood at the cottage door, waving to them as they left. After they had been walking for ten minutes or so, Angel saw that 'Liza-Lu was silently weeping and he took her hand as he had done when they left Melbury on the day of Tess Durbeyfield's execution.

To his surprise, she pulled it away with a jerk, and stood still, looking at him.

She shook her head, and said, 'No, Angel, please do not take me by the hand. Yesterday we did like this for comfort, but today I truly know Tess is dead, and I feel it 'ud be wrong for me to take your hand. It is too like sweethearts. And you know we are not sweethearts.'

Angel looked at her sorrowfully, 'No, dear 'Liza-Lu, we are not sweethearts and I am too sad at heart to think of sweethearting now, but I must tell you what dear Tess said to me before they took her away, when we were happy together, in an old empty house in the wood, for a day and a night. It was the one and only time in our life together – that one day and that one night – when we were happy and loving and told each other all that was truly in our hearts.

Tess said if they arrested her, and if they hanged her for killing that vile man, D'Urberville, I should marry you, growing to a woman now, old enough to marry and so like her, though good, she said, as she was not.'

'But she was, she was good. If anyone ever was good, she was. There was no woman in this whole wide world better than our Tess, but wicked things were done to her. First she went away to work for all our sakes, and that wicked man deceived her and ruined her, and she had her little baby that she christened her very own self. I was there, Angel, with Aby and Hope and Modesty and the little ones, but it was me held the big Prayer Book open for Tess to read all the christening service. She had to hold the little baby in her arms, and it was me asked her what she was going to call him, because he didn't have any name at all till he fell so ill and she wanted to christen him.'

'She never told me that. She told me – that dreadful night – our wedding night – when she told me her story, so truthful, so trusting, thinking I would understand, as I should have understood … oh God.' There was a sob in Angel's voice. 'There were many things she didn't tell me, because I was a hard man, and I cast her off. I knew she had a baby. She told me that, but I didn't know about the christening. I didn't know it was a boy. I didn't know its name. She never said its name. I didn't ask. I was only thinking of myself.' He looked at 'Liza-Lu. 'What was the baby's name?'

Her eyes grew moist. 'Sorrow, his name was Sorrow, that was the name she chose. Yes, a sad sad name for the little boy. Yes, it was a boy. She said it just came into her head when I asked her what name it was she had picked out. She hadn't thought. And when I asked her about his name she looked surprised, then – all in a flash – she said the name Sorrow.'

'Was that a name for a child?'

'Liza-Lu flushed, ''Twas a true Bible name, so 'twas, out of the book of Genesis, the Scripture that we all read in the village school and heard in church. Jacob's own wife Rachel named her child the son of sorrow, before she died. Tess told us the name and later on she explained it all and told me the story. I didn't know it before, but Tess did. She said poor Rachel died after she had her baby, but with us it was the other way round, and it was the poor little baby died. Tess gave him a true Scripture name, indeed she did. I remember how she looked when she read the service, and I tell 'ee she looked like an angel, holier than any man in the church, as she looked at the Prayer Book in my hands and read the service, and sprinkled the water and made a big cross sign over him, and told us all when to say "Amen" after she said the words. I'll never forget how she looked after she had finished and we all said "Amen" at the end. She didn't look like our Sissy at all. She was looking up, high up, far away from us all. Then she looked back at the little baby, and she hugged him to her and she cried, very much. She loved him very much, Tess did. It was because he fell ill that she wanted to have him christened, but our father said he wouldn't have the church people in the house, even if they had been willing.' She bit her lower lip.

'Before he was ill, it was I who used to look after the baby, because I was the eldest after Tess, and she 'ad to go out every day and work on the harvest stooking, almost as soon as it were born, and I used to carry it out to the field where she was working with the other binders so that she could suckle it. But the little baby sickened and died, and the cruel church people wouldn't let her bury it in the churchyard. And then she went away where nobody knew about it all, to the dairying in the place where she met you, but then 'ee married her and then left her straight after, and went off to foreign parts. She told me all about it. She worked hard, she did, and then my mother fell sick and my father raved and ranted about our great ancestors, and said it was beneath his dignity to work, and I didn't know what to do, with all the little ones, so I traipsed all the weary way from Marlott to Flintcomb Ash, more miles than we walked yesterday, and Tess came back home and we two and Abraham worked hard at nights weeding and digging and planting the allotment-plot, and then the fat round father's heart finished growing right round it – the doctor said so – so all of a sudden he dropped dead. And the house was for his life and so we had to go, there was no money and nowhere to sleep, except the family tomb with all the Durbeyfield – D'Urberville – ancestors, where mother took us, and what could Tess do to feed us and shelter us but go back to him, back to that wicked man. He said she belonged to him and he said you wouldn't come back. She told me she didn't know what to do. I cannot bear to think of it, indeed I cannot.'

'Liza-Lu sat down on the grass at the verge of their path and cried as if her heart would break, loud and bitter sobs, but she kept on speaking as she wept, in little bursts of story.

'And then you came back, and she always loved you, and she killed him with the kitchen knife, that wicked man! And you two went off but they went after you and found you, then of course they took her and hanged her, and we saw that black flag, but if you call her wicked for killing him, then I am wicked too, because I am glad she killed him, I am glad he is dead. I will never call dear Tess wicked, because I know she was never wicked at all. I know what happened. She was good.'

She rubbed her hand across her eyes, got to her feet and looked straight at him, new sobs rising as she spoke, her long thin legs below the short skirt, in her awkward limbs and trembling lips still a child, but all woman in her voice.

'No, no, no, Angel Clare. I can never marry 'ee, no matter what she said and no matter what you want. Never. She was good, she was the best woman I ever knew, and you could never have found a better wife, not in this life, though you did not know it. Never. But I will help you, for her sake. And for my mother and my brothers and sisters. You were hard to her, but I am willing to go with you and help you, and I will find work where you find work, but we will be brother and sister, as we should be, and as the parson would say we should be, and as I want us to be. I am not Tess, and I will not ever be your wife, only your friend and your sister. We will find work, and when I have saved a bit of money I will go back to mother and the children and help them.'

'But 'Liza-Lu, you know it was her dearest wish, and her very last wish.'

'It may have been her wish at the time, but that was when she was afraid and sick at heart, and going to be hanged by the neck by cruel men, and surely in need o' comfort and hope. Now she is in heaven she understands that I cannot do what she wished. And it will not be her wish any more. She knows better now.'

Angel began to speak, but stopped and shook his head.

'Oh, I know you do not believe there is a heaven, or that she is happy there. She told me that, and she told me that because she loved 'ee and wanted to believe what 'ee believed, for you was a wise and educated man, she thought – but between times, not all the time, she said – that perhaps you was right and there was no God. And perhaps there was no heaven where you two would meet again and be together after you died, as she wished and wished with all her heart. She said this was a worse thought and a bitter thought to have in her mind. But I am not as clever as you or as clever as dear Tess. Yes, she was clever, though not book-learned like you, though she was a good scholar and got to Standard Six. None of the rest of us was as clever as her. I remember how she looked like an angel when she read out the words from the Prayer Book I held open before her as she was holding the little baby who died, whose name she got from the Bible. And I truly believe she is a spirit now, and with her little baby, Sorrow, but they are not sorrowing any more, no, but with the angels in heaven, happy as she deserves to be at last, and I believe she can see you and me, and she understands now that I cannot marry you. She knows better now. I will help 'ee as best I can, and my mother and my little brothers and sisters too. If one day I meet a good man who will love me and help my family, I will love him and marry him, but if I do not, I will be glad to stay with mother and the children, and work hard for them, like Tess, until I die. And I will never forget Tess, because she was the best and the cleverest and the truest woman I have ever known.'

Angel Clare looked at the tall budding creature in the dress she had long grown out of, a girl still, slighter than Tess, her cheeks, lips, and body less rich and rounded but with the same full pouting red lips and those same beautiful dark eyes looking earnestly at him, not blue, not black, not green, that he had seen and loved in Tess. After a long pause he spoke.

'Well, my dear 'Liza-Lu, perhaps you are right after all and I was wrong. I will go with you to my mother and father – they have faith in God and heaven, like you – and I will tell them the whole story, and I believe they will receive you kindly and be your friends, and they will lend me money and then we will go back to your family and all move away from that place and help them to find work and keep a roof over their heads. Tess asked me to teach you, and I will do so as far as I am able, but I am not wise, and there are far better teachers than I am, so you shall go back to school. You will get to Standard Six like Tess, and if you work hard, and I help you, you can be a pupil teacher. I promise I will work for you and the others, and I will be your brother, as I truly am your brother-in-law. You shall have a better life than poor dear Tess, I promise you. I too can never forget her. We will remember her together. You are right and I was wrong. I was not a good husband to her. I was hard, and shut my heart against her when she told me the truth, though she had only done what I had done myself – less, far less, because she could not help herself. But never mind that now. Tess was a good and faithful wife to me, and you are right, she was the best woman I have ever known, a true woman, and a pure woman. We will remember her always, and love her memory. Yes, you are right. As I hear you speak and as I look at you now, I see too you have your life before you, and I have only error and misery behind me. My marriage ended in a good woman's hanging. It is for me to help you, if I can, but not to join my bitter life with your young hopeful life. Take my hand now, 'Liza-Lu, but only like a sister taking her kind brother's hand, because you are tired and the next village is a long way from here. Dry your tears.'

He looked at 'Liza-Lu questioningly, and when she rubbed her hand across her eyes and nodded her head, he took her by the hand, and as they slowly followed the sheep-track over the steep hill she did not take the hand away.

Note

After Tess begs Angel to marry her sister, just before she is arrested for murdering Alex d'Urberville, Hardy leaves the couple walking away together, hand in hand, like and also unlike, Milton's Adam and Eve: he does not tell us whether Angel proposes marriage. I have followed the couple a little way on their journey to allow 'Liza-Lu a personal liberation.

Also by Barbara Hardy

LITERARY CRITICISM

The Novels of George Eliot: A Study in Form
The Appropriate Form: An Essay on the Novel
The Advantage of Lyric
Dickens, The Later Novels: Writers and their Work
The Moral Art of Dickens
The Exposure of Luxury: Radical Themes in Thackeray
Tellers and Listeners: The Narrative Imagination
Charles Dickens: Writers and their Work
Particularities: A Reading of George Eliot
Forms of Feeling in Victorian Fiction
A Reading of Jane Austen
Narrators and Narration: Collected Essays
Henry James, The Later Novels: Writers and their Work
Thomas Hardy: Imagining Imagination
Dylan Thomas: An Original Language
George Eliot: A Critic's Biography
Dickens and Creativity

BOOKS EDITED

Middlemarch: Critical Approaches to the Novel
Critical Essays on George Eliot
Daniel Deronda by George Eliot
The Trumpet Major by Thomas Hardy
Not So Quiet... by Helen Z. Smith
London Rivers (with Kate Hardy)

AUTOBIOGRAPHY, FICTION AND POETRY

Swansea Girl
London Lovers
Severn Bridge: New and Collected Poems
The Yellow Carpet: New and Collected Poems

Victorian Secrets

Victorian Secrets is an independent publisher dedicated to producing high-quality books from and about the nineteenth century, including critical editions of neglected novels.

FICTION

A Mummer's Wife by George Moore
The Autobiography of Christopher Kirkland by Eliza Lynn Linton
The Blood of the Vampire by Florence Marryat
The Dead Man's Message by Florence Marryat
Demos by George Gissing
East of Suez by Alice Perrin
Henry Dunbar by Mary Elizabeth Braddon
Her Father's Name by Florence Marryat
The Light that Failed by Rudyard Kipling
Twilight Stories by Rhoda Broughton
Vice Versâ by F. Anstey
Weird Stories by Charlotte Riddell
Workers in the Dawn by George Gissing

BIOGRAPHY

Notable Women Authors of the Day by Helen C. Black
The Perfect Man: The Muscular Life and Times of Eugen Sandow, Victorian Strongman by David Waller

For more information on any of our titles, please visit:

www.victoriansecrets.co.uk

Lightning Source UK Ltd.
Milton Keynes UK
UKOW030519261111

182731UK00003B/7/P